ꝥRAGMENTS

Alora's Tear, Volume I

NATHAN BARHAM

BARHAM INK
MOSCOW IDAHO USA

Table of Contents

For Kel, because it has always been about you and me.

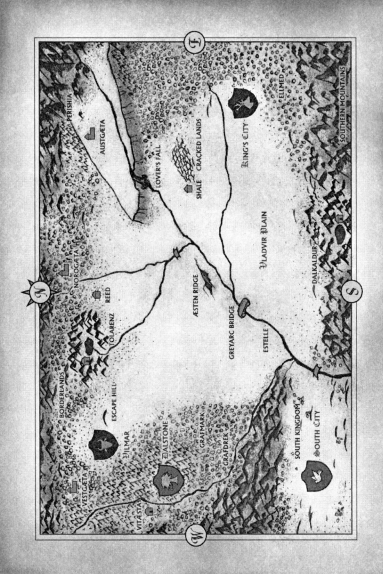

FRAGMENTS

Prologue

Thunder rolled across a deep velvet sky as distant as the grumbling of the gods, and to the young man hidden within the sticky needles of fir and spruce, just as irrelevant. When a sheet of scattered raindrops peppered the forest floor, he knew that the time had come. For several hours now, against orders and beyond help, Askon had lain silent and still as death, the scent of conifer swirling all about him. In the darkness and driving rain, his eyes—one green and one brilliant blue—burned with reflected firelight.

Ghastly shadows danced around the bonfires some fifty yards from his hiding place. He breathed deeply. His stillness was not that of peace or calm; it was a volatile cocktail of deep-seated rage mingled with raw adolescence. Excitement, bloodlust and a hunger for control simmered below the surface. Much training, daydreaming, and ridicule had led him here, to the rain-soaked perfume of the thicket.

Two days earlier, King Codard's son, Edward, had been captured. A boy new to manhood—like Askon himself—the prince had chosen the role of scout in his father's army. He could have elected a life of luxury in the castle, but instead had enlisted like a commoner and thus arrived at the northwestern border-fort of Vestgæta. There, the army fought a protracted battle with creatures known as the Norill. When Askon had asked if the military unit would send a rescue party for Edward, the commanders had laughed.

> *"He's as good as gone."*
> *"That's what he gets for leavin' the castle walls."*
> *"Fine, Askon, throw your life away trying to rescue him. See who notices."*

The jeering voices of memory made Askon's decision for him. Honor was never easy to come by, and respect even more difficult to earn; but for someone like Askon it was near impossible. In the land of Vladvir those with even the slightest trace of elven heritage were given the title 'Half-elf'. Askon had more trace than most. By rescuing a captured prince, Askon stood to gain glory for himself, if not his people, and he could satisfy his sense of duty. The prince had chosen to enlist, and that deserved respect.

"See who notices," Askon muttered as the droplets rattled a drum-cadence against his deep green cloak. Beneath the hood, a tangle of brown hair dripped onto pointed ears. His face, in some ways angular and cold like those of his father's people, had also a roundness about the cheeks and chin that more closely resembled his mother and the humans of Vladvir.

A flash of lightning tore through the clouds. Askon rocked forward anxiously, his first movement for many minutes. His breathing accelerated. A sharp crack of thunder split the monotony of the rain. On and on it boomed as though someone had murdered the sky. All around the bonfire the sinuous shadows continued their dance.

"Filth," Askon spat as the thunder rolled away and the rain hissed in its place.

At the firelight's furthest edges, he could see the rough-hewn cages where they kept the prisoners. A day's worth of reconnaissance had taught him that the guards were few and distracted, the cages shoddily built, and the gates wound with twine. But the Norill were many. Like a writhing insect hive they squirmed from place to place, arms dangling low, knuckles nearly touching the ground. Shriveled animal skins and bleach-white bones served them for armor. Underneath, their gray, mottled bodies had shone with sweat. That had been while the sun still lit the blue-green valley; before the dark; before the rain; before the dance.

On it went until one by one the Norill slithered away from the dying flames. A chill wind swirled through the thicket, rattling the branches like bones, whispering through the trees like the last breath of a dying man. The once lurid flames cowered weakly in the wind, burning low; gasping tongues of fire licked out greedily.

Askon smiled. Two guards at the entrance. Those he thought he could slip past on the way in, but not on the way out. Two more straggled by the fire pit, probably drunk on whatever vile concoction they had consumed during the dance. And then the cage-guards, hopefully asleep or dozing. It didn't matter. His chance was singular and desperate. His two-colored eyes flickered once again; this time with a wild inner light. Without so much as the snap of a broken twig, he rose from concealment and sprinted across the darkened clearing.

As he slipped through the gap several feet from the entrance gate, Askon drew his sword with his left hand. A long, curved hunting knife glimmered in his right. Somewhere in the camp there was a clatter: brief, not a threat. Then once more the rain drizzled down, pinging against a cooking pot nearby. He rounded the flimsy lean-to that abutted the spiked wall. There, sleeping heavily, its crooked mouth dangling wide, sat a Norill fighter, five feet in stature. A snort and gurgle issued from the gaping mouth, and Askon made his first mistake.

Without a thought, Askon cocked back his right arm and drove the hunting knife deep into the creature's neck. Large moony eyes rolled in their sockets; flat, papery nostrils flared. He twisted the blade with a nauseated snarl, sickened by the Norill stench.

But the creature did not die. It shuddered violently then screeched, choked, and fell barking into the mud. Askon dove on the body, stabbing quickly: heart twice, neck once more. He stamped on the throat, and the Norill lay still, its mischief complete.

Quickly, shocked by his own ruthlessness, Askon dragged the corpse back behind the building where he had entered. He did not intend to return this way. By the time he reached Edward, the camp would be swarming like a dislodged wasp's nest. They would have to fight their way out through the gate. Askon had not accounted for alerting the Norill so soon. Cautiously, he crept along the wall past two more buildings then back toward the smoldering fire. As he peered out from his hiding place, he saw that one of the Norill had slogged its way from the fire pit to the shack where Askon had so sloppily dispatched his first target.

Time would soon be running out; Askon bolted across the open space between the row of buildings and the embers of the bonfire. There, a reeling Norill stared stupidly into the glowing coals as the rain popped and hissed on contact. When Askon collided with the fire-watcher, he made his second mistake.

The creature was small, almost a full foot shorter than Askon, but its wobbling posture belied a sturdy balance and sure-footedness. It did not go down with the ease Askon had anticipated. They crashed into the mud together and slid half a yard before grinding to a stop. The creature was already back on its feet. A foam of spittle and mud bubbled through its pointed yellow teeth. Bewildered by darkness, surprise and likely drunkenness, it twisted and flailed, searching for its attacker.

This time, Askon did not make a mistake, nor did he relish the Norill's death. Methodically, he fell upon the creature: a lunge, puncturing the lungs; a slash to the base of the neck; and two percussive stabs to the heart, whereupon it fell. Again, Askon dragged the body into the shadows. When he emerged, the creature that had followed the sounds of the first kill had returned. It inspected the area, appearing to look for its drinking-mate, but finding none. Stumbling slightly, it lumbered off to the south, deeper into the encampment.

Askon breathed a sigh of relief. Twice he had been lucky. Twice he had failed to follow the teachings of his childhood; the lessons of his military training. To expect survival of a third would be asking for death. Another peal of thunder boomed over the camp; the same tortured, wailing cry. Askon ran for the prisoners' cages, capitalizing on the noise, his boots slapping over the growing slop of mud below. He pulled up short, sliding a little, but stayed on his feet.

Before him lay a long row of wooden cages. In one, Askon saw the prince's scouting team. They were dead, probably long since, but in the darkness and rain Askon could not be sure. Piled over their corpses were their cloaks, King Codard's bright blue stag visible on the black cloth even in the darkness. In the next two cages Askon saw something he could not later bring himself to describe. The remains had been human, but only the most gruesome details revealed them as such. He flinched and turned away. At the end of the row, a huddled form breathed slowly. It looked asleep, but something wasn't right about the movement. It was the only cage with a living prisoner, and boasted the only guards. Circling behind, Askon approached the cell. To his surprise, the guards slept soundly, and he resisted the urge to kill them. Quietly he stepped to the rear edge of the cage.

"Edward?" he whispered.

No response.

"Prince of Vladvir? It's Askon of Tolarenz."

A wild-eyed face peered out from beneath the folds of its cloak. It was Edward. His dark features, in combination with the rain and the damp and the pallor of fear made him look as though he had gone mad.

"Is it so?" he gibbered.

"It is s—"

But Askon did not have time to finish. The guards had not been sleeping at all. Cold, clammy hands twisted his arm and shoulder. It seemed though that the Norill made mistakes as well, and Askon thanked the gods for it. He dropped the sword and stabbed up into the Norill's arm, nearly driving the hunting knife into his own shoulder. Then he deftly spun the blade and stabbed the second guard in the bottom of the jaw, slicing through the windpipe on the return. Askon turned again and retrieved his fallen sword, thrusting it deep into the first guard who writhed frantically on the ground. The second was already dead, its blood mixing with the mud and rainwater.

When Askon looked up, Edward seemed to have come to his senses. He stood now, still pale but upright in the cell. Askon made several strategic cuts in the twine wrappings that secured the wooden poles. Then he gripped the rear wall.

"Take a run at it," he ordered.

Edward backed toward the door, then gestured with his fingers: one, two…

He slammed into the backside of the cage while at the same time Askon pulled against it with all his strength. The creaking poles bent visibly and Askon heard several pieces of twine pop loose, but the cage held. Again Askon sliced at the twine in the hope that he wouldn't be forced to saw through every strand, and again Edward sprinted, shoulder first, into the back wall of his prison. This time the poles cracked at their base while the twine twisted loose. Askon cast the remains of the cage wall aside. Edward stepped forward.

"Thank you," he said, looking from side to side at the wreck.

Askon scowled. "I did only what I had to."

Edward made a rasping choke of a sound; Askon wondered if it was a laugh. "I hardly think anyone ordered you down here. If I had to guess, I'd say you grew tired of them taunting you."

Askon said nothing.

"I know of only one company in the king's service that has both a prince and a half-elf among their ranks. I have heard their talk. However, now is hardly the time for it. May I use one of your weapons? We will need them if we are to get out alive."

Askon looked first to his sword. Given to him by his father at his coming of age ceremony, he was sworn to honor it as an extension of himself. An elvish tradition, he could no more give the sword to Edward than he could shear off his own arm and lend it to the prince. So he flipped the hunting knife in the same effortless motion he had used when fighting the guards, this time with the hilt facing outward.

"If you lose this, you'll wish I hadn't saved you," he said with a grin.

By the time they reached the gate, nearly a dozen Norill had crowded around the narrow opening in the outer wall. To the south, behind Askon and Edward, an alarm sounded. The clatter awoke the entire camp. Eyes burning with a wild light, sword held high, Askon of Tolarenz charged the Norill at the gate with Edward, prince of Vladvir, at his side.

CHAPTER ONE

The Valley of Tolarenz

A gentle breeze caressed the grass. Cows and horses grazed in the distance, while smaller creatures moved through the fields and scuttled in the trees. The morning sun had just broken the horizon, its warm glow embracing the valley. Next to the scattered buildings, a round, smooth lake mirrored the sky. A stream snaked along the roadside, following it lazily to a narrow pass in the mountains that surrounded the town. Dragonflies swooped and flitted along the river, flashing vivid blues and greens when they stopped to hover.

The stone-paved roads were clear, except for one lone figure striding up the path. Cottages lined either side, short wooden structures with thatched roofs, none with a second story. Before every house, plants and trees sprouted in a myriad of differing designs and styles. Some walkways had lines of bright flowers, alternating blue and red. Others had squat, gnarled shrubs standing no more than a couple of feet from the ground. A unique centerpiece graced each of the gardens: a small pond with shining lilies, a latticework archway with hundreds of tiny rosebuds, a tree with strong branches to support flowers in hanging baskets. A few of the houses crawled with ivy interspersed with blue and white morning glory blooms. Every dwelling along the path seemed almost to have been grown rather than constructed.

The figure increased speed as it rounded a corner and headed west toward the final cluster of houses next to the lake. At the end of the path, a large building stood nearly twice the height of the homes around it. Heavy wooden beams protruded from the corners of the structure, and a vaulted roof stretched skyward. The woodwork was the finest the town had to offer. Intricate carvings encircled the many pillars: warriors with swords raised, musicians with lutes and harps, weavers and farmers and smiths at their work, and through it all, meticulous depictions of growing things.

Ancient trees framed the walkway and towered over the hall. Their branches embraced the sky in a welcoming dance for the approaching figure. Farther along, haphazard rows of shrubs and bushes grew in a seeming pattern of wilderness. Where their limbs had grown together, archways had been woven, making them akin to a series of living hallways. At the end of the path, and nearing the door of the hall, the flowers began. Every variety present in the home gardens was represented here: reds, blues, violets, and on and on. The figure passed them by, reached for the door handle, and stepped inside.

"Askon!" squawked the doorman nervously. "We have been expecting you, but I'm afraid Lord Caled is still in preparation. He should be only just a moment." The servant reached for Askon's cloak but missed and stumbled. Askon had already moved away.

"I'll wait out in the garden," he said and stepped back through the door.

In a hidden room at the rear of the hall, Lord Caled paced, deep in thought. There were no windows and only two entrances, both of which were kept secret to protect the town's most valuable citizen. The only illumination came through a skylight high above. An ornate carpet mirrored the day-lit sky on the dark wooden floor.

One wall was completely obscured by a heavy bookcase filled with volumes—a collection from which any and all townspeople could request a volume, so long as the missing book was properly catalogued by one of the servants in the main chamber. Each day, Caled retrieved the new requests and placed the returned items on the shelf. On the opposite wall, there was a simple oaken desk, papers and writing tools spread loosely across its surface. One particular stack, weighted down by an ink bottle, leaned precariously to one side. As Lord Caled passed, he subconsciously nudged the bottle back to safety before reaching for the silver chain that fastened his cloak. At its center was a bright green gem that he rolled between thumb and forefinger.

Behind him, in one of two soft, upholstered armchairs sat a man robed in purple deep enough to be mistaken for shadow. His hooded face was only partially visible. A thin finger rummaged through a plate of nuts and dried fruit. The other hand, blotched and wrinkled with age, clutched a smooth stone as purple as his robes. He tapped the plate rhythmically with a pointed fingernail, selected a nut, then cracked it noisily against the table.

"So?" his ancient voice croaked, as he picked through the broken bits of shell. "Will you tell him? Or will you remain alone?"

"I'm afraid it isn't that easy," said Lord Caled.

The man in the chair chewed thoughtfully for a moment. "Oh it's that easy. It's the decision that's difficult."

"Semantics. The decision is the task," Caled replied.

The old man discarded the broken shell and brushed his palm against his robe. "The difference between peace and war, riches and debt is often decided by semantics. I think they're worth debating," he said.

Caled wasn't convinced. "Whatever the words, how can I be sure that he should know?"

"You can't. That is what makes it a decision."

"I can't do this forever, Morrowmen. Eventually someone else has to step in."

The old man rose from the chair and swiftly crossed the room. He was now inches away from Caled's face. "Actually," he said, "you *could* do this forever. You've managed this far, haven't you?"

"That's not what I mean," Caled replied. "I'm feeling terribly old these days."

"Ha!" Morrowmen croaked. "You feel old? By the looks of you, I wouldn't guess anything more than thirty-five. Look at this face." He pulled back the hood to reveal sunken eyes and pallid skin that bruised and purpled around the sockets. The eyebrows were thin and sparse, just a few white hairs where they had once been heavy and dark. His cheeks hung limply and the wrinkles around his mouth were innumerable.

"You may look it, but I feel it," Caled said. "For you, time has moved on. You have changed. I have not. All these years, I've been fixed, unmoving." He turned his back to the ancient face.

"He's not ready," Morrowmen crooned in a quavering sing-song. "But it seems that you are. This choice is yours of course. My advice is to tell him everything and hope he accepts it."

Caled let out a long sigh. "I know he's not ready. It's too much to process all at once."

"Again, it's your choice to make."

Lord Caled emerged from the hidden room, his bright blue cloak whispering along the floor behind him. He strode, with purpose eerily similar to Askon's, through the hall toward the main chamber. At the innermost end sat a simple wooden arm-chair on a short dais. Next to the chair were two objects: an impeccably wrought sword marked with runes, and a short golden scepter with a large gem at its top. Caled reached for the scepter and continued along the soft red carpet that led from the main entrance to the back of the room. He stood confidently upon the dais, his sharp chin angled ever so slightly upward. In his right hand, the scepter swung idly.

"Call him in!" he shouted.

Askon stood impatiently in the garden. He ran his hands across a branch and listened to the chirping birds as he moved. Beyond the birds, ever so faintly, metal pinged and clanged on metal. Smith-work. Muffled voices filled the streets as the town came alive with the morning sun.

The doorman laid a hand on his shoulder.

"Lord Caled will see you now, sir."

"Thank you," Askon said, and then added, "I hope he has had enough time to prepare."

"Sir?"

"Never mind."

As Askon left the bright sunlight of the garden and entered the shadowed hall, he was transported back into the far reaches of memory. They had excavated the heavy floor stones from a low bluff nearby. The building's four corner posts had each taken a team of men to raise and set. Garden plants and bushes had needed holes and then water; outer surface panels and columns had needed carving and engraving; the workers themselves had needed food and drink.

Askon also remembered the day that they officially opened the structure to the public. There was a ceremony and an inspiring speech from Caled about acceptance and togetherness. Even some of the more pessimistic elders had arrived to participate in the celebration. The project was an inarguable success, and the community only grew the stronger.

"Thank you for coming." Caled's formal yet friendly voice cut through the nostalgia. "I've been meaning to discuss some things with you for some time now. And I believe that you are ready to hear them. Please, come and sit." He motioned to a table and some chairs. As they sat, the doorman appeared with a pitcher of water and two full glasses.

Lord Caled began. "I have to start by saying that Tolarenz has no better friend than you. Not only did you help with the construction of the town as a boy, you've been a stalwart defender of the people and an excellent representative in Lord Codard's army." He lifted the glass and took a sip. "You've also spent quite a lot of time around here with me. We've been over city documents, disputes among citizens; you've even been present for discussions concerning the neighboring townships and cities. Most of Tolarenz' people never even leave this valley, let alone fight in an army that doesn't completely accept us."

Askon bowed his head. "Thank you, but I do only what I feel is required of me."

"Is it required then, to assemble a small force and follow a band of thieves to the borderlands? Is it required to go behind enemy lines to rescue those who would as soon name you villain as comrade?"

"Allies are allies. And one of them was the son of the king. So, I would argue that yes, it was required," said Askon.

Caled laughed. "It was more of a risk to save a friend, I'd say. You were lucky to get out alive. How long have you known Edward now?"

"Long enough," said Askon reluctantly.

"Indeed," said Caled. "Well, whether you accept it or not, you are one of Tolarenz' bravest and most outstanding citizens."

"But I—"

"Just take the compliment and listen. As I was saying, I have some things to discuss with you, and your standing in the city is what has led me to my decision." He slid Askon's glass across the table. Then he raised his own. "To your dedication," he said.

"To Tolarenz," said Askon.

The two men drank in salutation to the city. Askon's glass contacted the table first, producing a dull thud upon the smooth wooden surface. Caled's glass followed more softly. They looked across the table at each other, a staring contest in which it was obvious who would be defeated. After only a short interval, Askon was writhing in his chair with anticipation. A small, flat smile appeared on Caled's face.

"Out with it already," Askon said, exasperated.

The words seemed to hang in the air before continuing on through the long chamber and bouncing off the surrounding walls. Only on the echo did the message seem to reach Caled's ears. He considered it briefly, then looked to a painting on the wall.

"*The Raising of a City*. I've always thought that was such a fitting title," Caled said, leaning a little closer to the artwork. "Do you think the artist knew the title before he painted, or assigned it after?"

"Why don't you ask him? He's at work on another right now, just down the road. I thought you wanted to tell me something," Askon's eagerness nearly boiled over. Caled was willing to endure it.

"If you look closely, you can see the individual fingers wrapping around hammers and shovels. It's quite detailed." Caled was toying with him now, waiting for an outburst. It soon came.

"What are you waiting for?!" Askon snapped. "You sit here all day scheduling. A time for this, an appointment for that. I was informed of this meeting only yesterday, and I managed to be on time. You, on the other hand, keep me waiting in the garden and now ramble on about a painting you've seen every day since this hall was built. Get on with it, please!" Askon was panting now—and standing—his hands resting on the edges of the table.

"A time for everything indeed, Askon," Caled replied calmly. "All right, then. Have a seat. I suppose we can discuss this fine work at another time."

The response shocked Askon, though he should have expected it from Caled. Instead, the younger man had anticipated a similarly heated retort. Askon was suddenly painfully aware of the ridiculous stance he had taken at the table. He sat again and lowered his head.

"I apologize," he said.

"Thank you, but it is not necessary. I think patience will come with age for you." Caled took a breath and let it out slowly. "Alright. I have brought you here to give you some important information and to ask something of you as well. I think I will start with the request." He reached for his glass. "I have chosen you as my immediate successor. I'm sure you've heard the rumors; the town has been buzzing about it for quite some time. I am under the impression that the citizens agree."

"It is an honor," said Askon. "But why tell me this now? You hardly look old enough to be retiring already."

"Teaching someone to do this," he motioned to the room around him, indicating the tables, books, and papers that lined the hall, "will require a great deal of training. It will come in time. I may not look terribly old, but I think you'd be surprised to know the truth." He wiped a ring of condensation from beneath his glass. "You'll need to learn the systems for organization, formal procedures for public gatherings and appointments, and a great deal involving the cities outside this valley. There's so much that just doesn't come across in the common discussion. On the inside, it's all very complicated."

"I understand, but I'm enlisted in the king's army. We're leaving soon on an assignment. I can't just leave; they would have me charged with desertion."

Caled's voice was level and cool. "As I was saying, it's complicated on the inside. But with that sort of complication comes a bit of leeway that isn't available to the average person. I've already spoken with Lord Codard. We are in agreement that your service will end after this assignment."

"I see," said Askon. "And what if I refuse the offer?"

"That would be foolish, even for you."

Askon leaned forward to make a reply, but thought better of it and relaxed.

"Ah, wisdom begins to present itself," Caled said smiling. "We'll begin your formal training as soon as you return. I would be surprised if it was more than a month or two. The height of summer would be my guess, if I had to decide."

"What makes you so sure that I will return?" asked Askon. "It is a military assignment after all."

"Now you're fishing for compliments."

"Fair enough. What about the second item you wanted to discuss, the information?"

"I think that bit will need to be supplemented with food."

Caled clapped his hands and looked over his shoulder. The doorman reappeared immediately. He carried a wide silver platter, upon which rested two place settings and a delicious looking roast chicken with golden potatoes set all around. He set the platter in the center of the table and dispensed the flatware. Then, producing a careworn carving knife, he went about removing both legs and placing them on the plates. He made a few well-practiced slices, dividing the breast evenly, and stepped away from the table, gesturing toward the potatoes as he moved: a signal that the two men should help themselves. He bowed subtly, turned, and walked out of the room.

Askon breathed deep and reached for fork and knife, reversing their positions. He lifted a forkful. The two enjoyed the meal in silence for a few minutes; the only sounds were those of silver scraping against plates.

When most of the original serving was nothing more than a pleasant memory, Askon reached for the platter and removed another slice of chicken. He set it on his plate and looked up at Lord Caled. "Now we've eaten. What is the second item?"

"I suppose we could begin," said Caled, resting his fork and knife neatly on his plate. "With your new position as my personal protégé, there are some important things you must know about the history of your people and the people of the other cities."

"I know everything that I need to. Our people are persecuted—hunted even—by those who fear our heritage. They believe that elves, even half-elves, are in some way bewitched, or do the bewitching."

Caled slid his plate aside and leaned forward, elbows resting on the table. "Yes, this is true. But a great deal more has been lost or covered up by those same people.

"There is a very old story that I'm sure you've been told, though I wonder if you ever really listened. Long ago, in a kingdom not far from here, two men vied for the love of a woman. Both were of high standing, though one was born to it and the other made so by accomplishment and heroism."

"Of course I've heard it," Askon scoffed. "It's a children's fairy tale."

Caled smiled and paused for a moment. "The high-born of the two, Telemicus, was betrothed to the beautiful Alora, and happily. But the hero, Heraphus, came to visit the castle and fell instantly in love with Alora as well. The two had a blissful, romantic evening together, but in the morning, Heraphus watched in sadness as Alora accepted Telemicus's formal proposal. He never knew her true intentions. She had accepted only to buy time until the two of them might escape."

"Is there a reason that you seem determined to retell the whole thing?" Askon interrupted. Caled glanced sidelong at him, acknowledging and ignoring his protest all at once.

"Instead, consumed by sorrow," Caled continued, "Heraphus made his way to the cliffside near the castle and leapt to his death. Some say he was caught and lifted by the gods to become the Mender of Hearts.

"Alora, upon hearing of her love's tragic end, wept for days, locking herself in the room that Telemicus had provided. On the evening of the third day, she rose from the bed, and one final tear fell from her cheek. It crystallized before hitting the soft pillow. And there it remained, a beautiful deep blue jewel that radiated a light of its own. She then climbed the same cliff and jumped. By direct order from Telemicus, the Tear remained untouched for many years. As most tell it, Heraphus descended and lifted Alora up to be amongst the gods as the Breaker of Hearts."

Askon tapped his fork against the table. "Yes, it is a sad story. But I've heard it many times. As have all the children in Tolarenz. Even most of the men in my company know it," he said. "But what does this have to do with me or with running the city?"

"Oh yes, it is a very common story," Caled said thoughtfully, lifting his eyes again. "It concerns us because the story is true."

Askon was incredulous. "How can we possibly know if those people existed? It was so long ago."

"We know, because Alora's Tear is real," said Caled, his face grave.

"Is it?" Askon's sarcasm was palpable. "Well then, it's supposed that the Tear has all sorts of magical properties. There are stories about it. It must be true."

Caled laughed and leaned back in his chair. "There is much truth in jest," he said. "The Tear does have some properties that you might call magical."

"No," Askon said, indignant. "It's bad enough that people all over the kingdom think we practice magic. How can you suggest that we pursue something like this? Even if we had Alora's Tear—which I'm not yet convinced is even real—whatever power it has would only make our situation worse!"

"That is also true." Caled rose from the table and pulled his cloak away from the chair. He marched down the hallway, thumping the golden scepter against his hand. Askon pushed his own chair back clumsily and fell into step next to Caled. They walked a short distance, passing several well-detailed paintings in the same style as *The Raising of a City* before Caled began again. "What does the Tear have to do with us?" he asked himself aloud, then directed his gaze at Askon. "Do you know how the elves came to be in this world?"

It was a serious question; Askon paused to compose his answer. "I would have to guess that we have always been here, though I know of no pure elves living, nor have I heard of any.

There are the half-elves of Tolarenz and those who wander. I've seen them stalking the borderlands."

"Well," Caled said, wrapping his arms and the scepter behind his back, "there you are incorrect and correct respectively. To rephrase, you are correct that there are no pure elves living. But you are incorrect in your assumption that the elves were, and are, an original part of this world."

Askon stopped, "I suppose there's a story for that as well?" he said. Caled continued down the hall toward the dais.

"There is, and a long one. But there is no reason to overburden our first meeting. It will suffice to say that Alora's Tear is the key. It is how the elves entered this world and one reason why the pure no longer remain." Caled's voice dropped and his smile flattened into a tight-lipped frown. He straightened to his full height, quietly composing himself. "I think that will be enough until you return from your assignment. Go and serve Codard well. He will be hard-pressed to find a fitting replacement."

Question upon question circled Askon's mind, and the words began to push toward the surface. He opened his mouth to speak. Caled cut him off before he could begin.

"Just say 'thank you' and tend to your assignment. There will be more than enough time for questions."

Askon gave a quick bow. "Thank you, sir. I will return as soon as possible."

His every stride echoed in the hall as he let himself out. Behind him, Lord Caled stood watching, the golden scepter glinting in the half-light. His hand moved to his neck where, between thumb and forefinger, he turned the green gem over and over, its fine chain twisting and untwisting.

CHAPTER TWO

Home

Dazzled by the midday sun, Askon raised a hand to his face. He stood for a moment on the steps while his eyes adjusted. When he lowered his hand, he still had to squint into the lush garden.

"Leader of the city," he said to himself. A smile spread across his angular face. "But to follow Caled. Those are long strides to match."

A rustling sound caught his attention. He peered down the path, expecting a bird or squirrel, but saw nothing. It came again, only this time behind him. He whirled back around: still nothing. Listening carefully, he took a few wary steps down the path. When the breeze through the garden greeted him with a hiss, he straightened and, realizing how ridiculous he would look to someone passing by, resumed his walk through the woven arches.

A few feet before the path intersected with the road, the sound came again: *scrape, rustle, silence.* Askon froze, tension building in his legs and feet. *Crack…*

With startling quickness, Askon leapt between two waist-high bushes and scanned left to right. Another shrub farther into the garden jittered noisily. He made ready to pounce. But before he could move, the bush swayed to one side. A soft giggle and the patter of light footfalls receded into the distance.

"Líana," he muttered and rolled his eyes. He crossed the last few feet of the town hall garden and emerged onto the main path. Others in the town surely knew about his coming change of position; he hoped that they hadn't been watching as he thrashed about in the brush.

Founded by a group of half-elves and humans, the settlement had begun as a haven for the former. The humans who sympathized with them were in similar danger, though to a lesser degree. Half-elves were considered deceptive, dangerous, totally alien from the human race, and were often attributed with pre-posterous magical abilities. As time passed, Tolarenz added many differing groups to its population. There were varied spiritual theorists, scholars, political dissidents, and even a few outlaws. Yet, in spite of being removed from their original cities or lands, all seemed to coalesce in the green valley with the little river.

Feeling as though all eyes were upon him, Askon made a point to address the townspeople as he passed. The first house he came to, also the largest on the row, was that of Roland, the smith. It was from here that Askon had heard the clatter of metal while he waited for Caled. Roland's garden was stark and simple. There was greenery, of course, but the plants were few and the grasses grew high and feathery. Around the door, a few potted flowers dangled, but the real display pieces were their vessels, painstakingly wrought from blackened iron. Askon rounded the side of the house and made his way toward the ringing anvil.

Roland was a broad-shouldered bear of a man with a laughing face. He stood much taller than Askon, even while hunched over the forge. He lifted a glowing piece of iron from the flames and pounded it flat amidst a shower of orange sparks. Askon shielded his face and waited for the smith to place the iron back in the fire.

"What brings you my way this morning, Askon?" Roland said, wiping his forehead with a dingy cloth that appeared to have, at one time, been white.

"Just passing through and thought I'd say hello," Askon replied. "Maybe it's the sound of your hammer. Like some sort of birdcall. It draws me in."

"Ah, that's a bit o' nonsense," snorted Roland. "You been in to see Caled. He's told you what we've all been thinkin'. By rights, You'll be takin' his place."

Askon leaned against the side of the house. "You couldn't be more right. With all the ringing and banging with that hammer, I would think that your hearing would be worse, not better."

"Talk in this town's louder than five forges, as a rule." Roland winked, and turned back toward the anvil. "I think it's a sound choice by Caled. Couldn't've picked it better myself even. Congratulations and all that, but I need to be gettin' back at it." He jostled the iron amongst the glowing coals.

"Thanks Roland, I'll talk to you later. But I'll be leaving on assignment soon."

"Mind you aren't gone long."

Back on the main path, Askon's mind wandered again. Alora's Tear was real. He tried to brush the thought away with a small snort of a laugh, but it persisted. If such an artifact actually existed, its possessor would gain nearly limitless influence. If a leader could claim that he held the Tear, people from every end of Vladvir would come to be near it. Some said it could heal the sick, others that it could be used to conjure food, and still others told tales of the Tear as a great weapon of war.

"Does he know where it is?" Askon asked himself. "And if he does, why not tell me?"

The gravel popped under his boots, and the sun beat down on his back as he considered the question. The heat was mild, as it always seemed to be at this time of year. Roland's ringing hammer receded, and Askon passed the clothier and leather workers. He waved kindly and winked at one of the ladies busy at the loom. Then it was the mill next to the winding river and Eric the miller and his daughter Grace, covered in flour, at work with sacks of grain. Farther along the path, small farmhouses with collections of chickens or sheep rose up from the personalized gardens. Some indicated the family business, as did Roland's. Others purposefully contrasted the families' workday pursuits.

Beyond the farms, two buildings stood twice again as far from the town hall. The first was Askon's own home. The other was the home of the falconer, Halan. Not only was Halan the last of the villagers in Askon's tour, the two also had unresolved business.

Everything in and around Halan's home seemed tailored to the creatures he kept. The trees were tall with many bare, solid branches to act as perches and roosting places. Wood shavings from the carpenter's shop back in town littered the surrounding grounds. The sheer number of birds was startling. Some hopped from branch to branch along the walkway toward the door, and others, too noble to stoop to such childish games, merely watched like feathered gargoyles until Askon was out of sight.

One such creature, a sable gray merlin who had originally been perched amongst the larger peregrines, glided from tree to tree, stopping periodically to pick through the brown and white feathers at its breast. It followed Askon step for step as he approached the fork in the narrow walkway.

To one side was the falconer's home and a long dock that jutted out over the lake; on the other, the pathway led to the ramshackle mews. Askon passed it by and headed for the water. The merlin swooped fluidly along the ground behind him. On the dock, a figure stared across the lakeside, watching the birds of prey circle and dive.

"Halan?" Askon called. He continued out onto the wooden planks, his steps echoing between water and wood beneath the platform.

"Askon," Halan said. "Marten and I have been waiting."

Halan, who was half a head shorter than Askon, appeared every bit an elf, though even he was not fully pure. The long straight hair, lengthened ears that extended out to fine points, sharp features, slight build, and brilliant green eyes made his heritage unmistakably clear.

"Aren't they just inspiring?" He spoke with a soothing hum that helped to relax his birds. The sound had a similar effect on Askon. "Every movement is pure freedom."

Askon looked across the water and into the sky. There, in the glare of the midday sun, winged shapes of all sizes soared in great circles above them. He thought to himself how free they did look, but remembered that they were, in a way, Halan's captives. Askon lowered his eyes to the opposite shore. There he perceived his own measure of true freedom. The people of Tolarenz moved through their daily chores, some studying the arts and others partaking in more menial tasks. Warm pride swept over Askon. The people of Tolarenz were happy and free, and soon they would be in his charge.

"They are indeed inspiring," he said.

Taking Askon's meaning, the falconer turned and started back toward the mews. "You're here for Marten," he rumbled. "He has spent most of the day in the trees on the outside of the property. He generally prefers to associate with the peregrines. They protested at first, but I think he's proven his worth to them."

"Heh, that sounds like him all right," Askon replied. "I take it he has fully recovered then?"

"He has, but you should try to keep him from being too active. His wings aren't quite ready for full-time hunting just yet. You can take him home, though."

The merlin, who had been watching the conversation fixedly, dove from one of the dock's support pillars and flew in a wide circle just inches from the surface of the lake, so close in fact, that each flap of his wings sent water rippling behind him. When he had finished his demonstration of recovery, he fluttered back up and perched lightly on the leather pad that rested on Askon's shoulder.

"Feeling better, I see," Askon said, smiling. The bird bobbed his head in response and looked out across the water. "Thank you for your help, Halan."

"Always a pleasure."

Askon started toward the main road. The shadows had lengthened a bit, and the air was still and warm. He turned to the bird sitting on his shoulder. "Go on then," he said and shrugged abruptly. "You know you want to."

As if he had been waiting for permission, Marten rocketed up and away from his master, back amongst the peregrines. He addressed each, then circled the tops of the trees and came flashing down along the path, finally alighting back where his flight had begun. Askon watched the whole affair silently and continued toward the main path. With Marten at rest on the shoulder guard, Askon relaxed, his mind wandering again to the responsibility that would soon be his. And there it was again, a soft scraping sound: slight, almost imperceptible.

Scrape…crack…swish…

The sound came from behind him, amid a row of bushes that clung near the roots of the trees. He stopped, hearing only the soft flutter of Marten's feathers near his ear. But unlike earlier in the garden, Askon was ready. Like lightning, so fast that Marten had to take to the air, Askon's left arm plunged into the rustling leaves. After a short struggle, it emerged with its prize. Askon's fingers clasped tightly around a thin green shirt, upon which cascaded a mop of golden blond hair whose owner was currently thrashing furiously in an attempt to escape.

"Caught," said Askon reprovingly. "You've broken rule number one, Líana."

The whirling mass of hair stilled. "I know," it whined from beneath. "Don't get caught." Askon released her, and she pulled the long blond locks back behind her head. "But it wasn't fair, you're bigger and stronger than me."

"Bigger and stronger than I, if you don't want to sound like a kitchen servant," Askon said. "And it's nonsense anyway. Marten knew you were here when we left the dock, and he's neither bigger nor stronger."

The little girl scoffed and glared at the merlin. His eyes darted from tree to tree innocently. Líana kicked hard at a half buried stone. She was fair skinned, much fairer than Askon or either of his parents, and at ten years old stood a few inches higher than most of the boys her age. She was thin, but not frail, and though her hair and skin were light, she had a tough earthliness about her that seemed to come from deep within. Askon's mother had tried to direct her toward the pursuits of other girls her age, but it was hopeless.

She idolized Askon and followed him almost everywhere. Much to her pleasure, they even shared the same two-colored eyes; the only difference was that Askon's were blue and green from right to left, and hers blue and green left to right. When he was on assignment, she often set up camp somewhere outside of the town, as far from the house as their mother would allow. During these survivalist stretches, she could often be found whacking away at trees and shrubs, evidently practicing her swordsmanship, or spying on affairs in the town so that she might report the information when her brother returned home. Askon ruffled the hair on the top of her head.

"Let's go," he said.

The two walked back across the main path toward their home. At the top of the hill, the garden began. There were many trees, perhaps dozens; the family had lost count. But these were not the bare branched trees that lined the pathway to the falconer's mews, nor were they the broad oaks that covered the town hall garden. No tree here grew more than four feet high, and only two were actually planted in the ground. It was a forest of miniatures, small gnarled shrubs that made Askon feel like a giant striding through a tiny ancient woodland.

Hardy junipers began the garden, and the winding path led farther into rows of spindly red maple. The procession continued with figs and pines and elms, and ended with two squat oaks that thrummed with age and wisdom. These two sentries of the tiny grove were planted in the ground, the centerpieces of the garden. Every plant showed signs of impeccable care.

Askon admired the little forest as he and Líana walked along. Every few steps she would fall behind, trailing a hand along the tiny trees, careful not to overturn the pots in which they grew. Then she would take three steps to Askon's one to catch up.

Marten had flown ahead when they reached the main road and now perched atop the window ledge outside Askon's room, itself a rarity in Tolarenz, being on the second floor. When they were within a few yards of the door, Líana broke into a full sprint. By the time the race had been declared, she had already grabbed the door and swung it open, announcing herself the winner in the same breath.

Inside, the entryway was lined with two parchment partitions framed in cherry wood. On the parchment were printed the words "peace" and "tranquility" in an ancient script that used single intricate shapes to depict words. Askon and Líana each removed their shoes before entering, a traditional practice that Líana despised. Still panting from the one-man race, she flopped onto a soft chair with a sigh.

Askon's family were upper class, though even a family of the highest social rank in Tolarenz would have seemed a collection of paupers to those in the wealthy districts of larger cities. In Tolarenz, social class was reflected in the care and maintenance of one's home and not necessarily by the amount of land or money that the family possessed. In fact, it was the observance of traditions such as removing shoes that kept Askon's family firmly within its rank. The only other property that showed the same determined consideration was the town hall itself, and that was cared for by a force of servants.

In the kitchen, Askon's mother worked a lump of dough over and over on a cutting board. She had a gentle smile and a round face fringed with dark brown hair. Her build was solid, though not overly large. Her most striking feature was her eyes: piercing blue like a sunlit sky and deep as a shadowed sea. It was a gaze that looked directly into the soul, and from which there was no place to hide.

And yet, Askon found it reassuring to be within her sight. Under her watchful eye, all pretense or facade was lightly swept away. She could *see* you, even when you didn't want her to, and those same searching eyes operated in reverse as well. When she would look upon him, Askon could see right through the shining blue to what lay behind, which was always warmth and light.

"Well Askon, what did Lord Caled have to say?" she asked. And then, "Líana, your feet do not belong on that table." In a moment the girl's feet were back on the floor, and from her mother's vantage point, she resumed an upright posture. Askon however, could see the indignant brows and widening frown. He smiled and leaned against the counter where his mother was working.

"He said quite a lot, and almost all of it important." He looked over his shoulder toward his sister, then up the stairs, and finally down the hall toward the back of the house.

"Your father is outside," his mother said. "A couple of his favorite maples have taken sick, apparently. He had them in the house earlier, but I put an end to that."

"I'd like for both of you to hear the news," said Askon, though he was uncertain of how much Caled would want him to reveal.

"Well, you can go get him," said his mother, with mild irritation. "But tell him from me that if he tracks that dirt back in, he'll be carrying it out by hand." The last word was punctuated with a *pop* as she lifted and dropped the dough back onto the cutting board.

The low porch that clung to the back of the house was shaded and cool. Askon could hear the insects buzzing as before, only now louder and more distinct: a bumblebee humming through the trees and flowers, a grasshopper clicking incessantly, a cricket chirping. One lived to chirp no more, as Marten landed heavily on Askon's shoulder, audibly crunching the victim in his beak.

Askon's father focused intently on two small, mostly-dead trees. He moved from one to the other with swift purpose. Both had been removed from their pots, their bare roots protruding from clumps of dirt. Above them, hanging on a lattice, were several pairs of black iron pruning shears. Below hung many other tools of various kinds. There were rakes and spades, hooks and tines, and yet more shears, each with a specialized purpose.

The two men stood for some time before speaking, Askon excited at the prospect of discussing his time with Caled, and his father too deeply involved in the well-being of the trees. At length, the latter relinquished the forked root-rake in his hand. Both exhaustion and invigoration coursed over the lines of his face.

His father's deep green eyes had an unmistakable intelligence about them, and in one look it was easy to identify which side of the family contributed the elvish traits. The pointed ears and pronounced cheekbones were signal enough to even the casual observer, but Askon's father was not one to allow even such an observer to be mistaken. Inside the house there was a thick, heavy book bound in fine leather and embossed with the family crest. This massive tome articulated the very finest minutia of Askon's family history. His father took great pride in his ability to trace his lineage back many generations. In fact, by way of past arranged marriages, he was as close as anyone in Tolarenz to being pure elven (with the exception, perhaps, of Halan the falconer, though that difference was negligible and often the subject of friendly argument).

"Father," Askon said formally, though he rippled with anticipation.

"I'm quite busy," his father replied concealing a smile. "I have important matters to attend to." He motioned to the two small maples.

"You see," he said methodically, "this one to my left was far too eager. His leaves came on very early. He was looking quite strong, but then a touch of frost bit him in the night. I'm afraid he'll have quite the battle in order to recover. If it weren't for my help, he would not have made it." He brushed one of the spindly branches softly below a new bud.

"This one," he continued with a wave toward the other plant. "This one has been scraggly from the very start. He came on in his own good time, waiting out the cold, choosing the right moment. He's not the prettier of the two, but he certainly has the best chance at filling out later on. He'll be around for sure this fall. As strong as the branches and buds on the first one look, he'll be lucky to be around in a couple of weeks."

Indeed the tree on the right looked the weaker of the two. Its leaves were thin and a bit brown around the edges, and none of its branches seemed thick enough to support leaves in any amount. But Askon had not come to discuss his father's trees.

"I have news," he said, this time with more eagerness than before.

"Oh, I see. Too important to listen to a lesson from the old man," his father said, picking up the rake and wiping it with an oiled cloth.

"No, I just—"

"You've been to see Caled," he interrupted. "What has he told you?"

Askon recounted the meeting, beginning with the meal and the discussion of the artwork. When he had explained Caled's cryptic remarks concerning Alora's Tear and the end of the pure elves, Askon came to his first question.

"What happened to them?" he asked, leaning against the workbench.

"Truthfully, I cannot say what their fate was," Askon's father began. "My grandfather was alive to see them go, but our family had parted from those of pure descent long before." He shifted against the bench, looking out on the warm afternoon. "He told us that human sadness did not have the depth to understand the sorrow of their passing. It was difficult for him to even discuss it. He said that everyone with elvish blood could feel it when the last of them left this world."

"You speak as though it happened all at once," Askon said.

"I do," his father replied. "Because that is the way my grandfather told it as well. He said it was like waking from a nightmare to find that it was no dream, and that the feeling remained, even after they had all gone." He pushed himself upright and took a step toward the door. He started to speak, but the words never reached Askon's ears. His mother and sister had just burst onto the porch.

"Well, that's about enough waiting," Askon's mother said irritably. "If you won't come to us, then we'll come to you. We're all here now. You can tell us what happened with Lord Caled."

Askon, feeling slightly irritable at the interruption, proceeded to recount the entire morning for his family. Discussing every point from his time spent waiting in the garden right up to the revelation that he would soon be the new leader of Tolarenz, he spared no detail. By then, Líana was pestering a line of ants that marched across the porch. Upon hearing the news, she jumped up excitedly, scattering the ants in all directions.

They took turns hugging him and patting him on the back, though the thought of him leaving for another tour with Codard's army embittered the moment. The news was an unparalleled achievement for not only Askon, but the rest of the family as well. In all of Tolarenz' history, there had been only one leader. Now, the leadership would be passed on, and each of them thought that there could have been no better choice for the position.

The celebration went on for some time. Askon's mother brought refreshments and food from inside, and the family took turns considering the possible steps the new leader might take. Nothing was left undisturbed, from high philosophy to limitations on gossip, to curfews for young children (a current rule that Líana vehemently opposed). This sort of talk continued until the sun moved to the very rim of the little mountains that encircled the valley. When the sunset faded, Askon's mother and sister went back inside.

"There is something that you should have, I think," his father said after they had gone. "It was given to me by my grandfather."

He turned and stepped through the door. Askon was left standing outside in the quickly cooling evening air. The crickets had taken the lead in the insect chorus and now drowned out all other sound. Marten, who had tired of the talk long before, was perched at one corner of the roof, peering down onto the fields, awaiting any creature brave enough to move in the dim light. A few minutes passed before Askon's father reemerged carrying a small leather-bound volume of perhaps a hundred pages. The family crest was hand painted on the faded black cover. He placed the book into his son's hands and covered them with his own.

"These are your great grandfather's writings. Maybe they can answer questions which I cannot." He smiled. "If nothing else, they will keep your mind busy while you are on your next assignment. Good night, and again congratulations."

Askon's father went back inside and did not return. In the deepening dark, a shiver crawled from the base of Askon's heel up his spine to his neck. He shook his head and shoulders. Above him, stars appeared in the blackness; first one, then another, and another, until tiny glittering points of light blanketed the sky. Askon turned his back on them, brushing his boots against the mat, and followed his father into the house.

CHAPTER THREE

Shadows in the Dark

They came in the night; silent forms gliding along the grass and up the hill. They swept through the garden soundlessly. Even the falcon perched on the second story neither saw nor heard them. Single-file they went under the stars, past the little trees to the door. A sound disturbed the silence, like pieces of broken glass grinding together. Whispers. There was a long pause. The group parted, two on each side, blacker than the darkness, and one in the center facing the door.

Bang!

The heavy fist against solid wood seemed to shake the whole house. It shattered the quiet of the valley, then died as quickly and forcefully as it had come, one piercing sound in the dead of night.

Marten took flight and circled high above the house. The forms stood motionless at the door, heads bowed. Seconds passed and small sounds issued from inside: rustling, shuffling, footsteps.

Bang!

Another burst of sound came, though the night seemed more prepared now, the shock less. The group at the door rocked from side to side, again voicing that dry, crackling whisper. Time was up.

The central form pushed the door open. The lock picked, it swung inward, defenseless on its well-oiled hinges. Wasting no time, the blackness swept from the doorstep to the inside of the house, fanning out as they entered. Moonlight reflected off crystal goblets in a cabinet across from them. The leader—the tallest of the group—moved toward the staircase and began to ascend.

One step at a time, head lowered, the figure crept toward the landing. It paused two steps from the top, scanning the opening to the second-story hallway. The others looked up in unison, shadowed faces revealing nothing in the darkness.

The leader peered into the hallway. Suddenly there came a flash of brilliant silver. The figure tumbled sprawling to the foot of the stairs. A body was on him almost before he landed, pinning him to the ground. Icy steel pressed at the veins pulsing in his exposed neck.

Dazed, the figure could neither move nor speak, but his assailant, Askon, had words to spare.

"Stand back!" he barked to the remaining intruders. "Drop your weapons!"

The figures stepped away, hands in the air.

"Show yourselves," Askon shouted. "Or this one won't live to speak." He pressed down hard on the man's throat with the long, curved hunting knife. The captured leader began to writhe beneath the blade.

"Say something," Askon demanded as he held the man to the ground, the knife edge threatening to slice through the thin layer of skin.

"Askon?" His father's voice came calm and low. A lantern swung from his hand, the stairway awash with its yellow light. "You've woken your sister. Your mother is putting her back to bed. Why are you shouting?" The newly revealed scene was anything but what Askon had expected. The light uncovered a gasping face, one that he recognized immediately. He released his grasp.

"John?" he said astonished, pushing himself upright. "What is wrong with you? Why would you break into my house?" The sprawling victim choked and coughed, doubling up on the floor.

"Sir, we were told to retrieve you immediately," came the voice of one of the others. "When you didn't answer after our knocks, we suspected the worst."

"We thought... somebody might've..." the figure on the floor rasped and pulled himself upright against the wall.

"Broken in?" Askon finished incredulously, his hands still trembling from the rush of adrenaline. "So you did just that."

"We've got orders to bring ya to our campsite as quick as possible," John said, coming again to his senses and rubbing his neck where Askon's knife had so recently rested. He swallowed hard. "There's a Norill colony swarming up the hill from Austgæta. But we can talk about it on the way. There's half a swarm of our own right now just outside of the valley. If we hurry, we might reach Austgæta in a few days' time."

"Typical," said Askon, annoyed. "Could they not have sent a message ahead?"

"We *are* the message."

The moments that followed were a whirlwind; what would usually have taken hours, compressed into minutes. Provisions were collected, clothing made ready, and medical supplies as well.

Askon's parents busied themselves in a similar way, moving quickly through the house, making ready for their son's departure. On one pass, his mother might be carrying loaves of bread or salted meats. On another, his father presented bandages and ointments. The army had its own supplies, of course, but soldiers commonly preferred the reminders of home.

For a while, John and the rest stood watching with arms folded as Askon and his parents made ready. John sighed heavily and shifted from one foot to the other. Askon's mother shot him a glare. He shrunk like a wilting flower and waited quietly. When Askon's gear had been fully collected, only John remained inside, now and then reminding Askon of the immediacy of their errand.

"You've got enough there for yourself and more," he was saying while Askon put the final touches on his pack, "unless you're bein' so kind as to set me up too."

"All right," Askon replied hurriedly. "That's everything, I think."

He crossed the room and lifted his cloak from the wall. Wrapping himself in the deep green fabric, he doused the lamp that sat near the window. When he reached down to shoulder the heavy pack, the only light remaining was the small lantern his father carried. It cast long shadows that leaned toward the door. John bowed his head and exited.

Askon curled a strong arm around his mother, who had not yet fully recovered from the shock of the forced entry. He hugged her, pausing for a moment, and then let go.

Only a few steps away, his father waited, holding something out before him. It was a thin, leather-bound book, his great grandfather's book. Gently, Askon pressed the volume between his hands and pushed it back toward his father.

"When I return," he said.

Both men bowed low. The door swung open again.

"Askon." John's voice was heavy and rough. There could be no more delay.

Askon stepped through the door and looked back over his shoulder. There were his mother and father, standing solemnly in the glow of the lantern, their faces covered in dancing shadows. His mother's striking blue eyes warm and proud, looking through his skin to his heart, and his father with his intelligent green gaze fixated on his son. They seemed small in the cold night air.

For a moment, Askon stood silent in the doorway.

"I know," said his mother, her eyes filled with concern, "just one more assignment."

"Don't worry about me," said Askon gently. "I'll stay safe." His father, with a nod, turned away. But his mother remained, and was still there when he closed the door behind him.

Five dark shapes flowed down the pathway as silently as they had come. An additional form shone green in the lantern light then faded to black. No sooner had they reached the main road than the pretense of seriousness lifted.

"Askon!" John said rather loudly, slapping him on the back. "You lazy sprite. You think you can come home and lay up for the rest of your days?"

Another on the opposite side of the line laughed deeply. "Askon? Lay up? He's probably been so buried in work that he doesn't even know that he left us yet."

"I can...lay up," Askon said, faltering.

This time the laughter pealed from everyone in the group. It bounded through the night, rolling over the hills and ricocheting off the nearby cliffs.

"Me an' the boys here were at the dice for a week after the tour," said John.

"Aye, and John actually did us all a favor for once and won some," said the second voice, and a tremendous cheer burst from the four lower ranking men.

"You'll recall I was kind enough to split it out even amongst us," John reminded him.

"That you did indeed."

Askon readjusted his pack. "I'm sure you put it to good use?"

"Oh did we," said one.

"I'll tell ya what we put it to," said another, reaching an arm around one of his fellows. "We put it to the tavern."

"You spent it on drinks?" Askon asked.

"Indeed we did, but not on ours," another said. "There were some upstanding and rightly attractive ladies 'round that place."

"I see," said Askon.

"Now that's what I call layin' up!" John boomed, and another riotous peal of laughter erupted from the group.

"Where are the girls now?" questioned Askon. "And the money?"

"Maybe you figured we all got married and bought houses," said John. "They're gone, as they should be."

"That's what I thought."

The group walked lightly down the road toward the flickering firelight of the camp, shoving each other as they went, John occasionally grasping his neck and rubbing the area where Askon had nearly strangled him. The stars shone above them, and a dark shape passed over the moon's uncovered surface. Marten had followed, but seemed content to keep his distance.

When the six companions reached the campsite, dawn already threatened to break over the mountains in the east. The sky went from unfathomable darkness to hopeful gray, and finally faint blue. Smoke rose in tendrils from the lowering flames of a half-dozen fires, and sounds of activity filtered through the air as the night's final watch woke the rest of the camp. Before they reached the other soldiers, John stopped. He put out a thick, strong hand, halting the group, and turned to Askon.

"We're glad to have ya with us," John said slowly. "But some o' the others, even the officers, don't like that we went out of our way to pick up one middle-ranking officer, and a half-elf at that."

"So you're telling me to expect the usual," Askon said flatly. His eyes fell on the nearby campsite, where people were pacing back and forth, folding tents and dousing fires. He asked himself which of these men would be unhappy at his arrival, then said, "I'm sure you've brought others from Tolarenz. Even if they're human, it's more than just one."

"Actually," muttered John, "all of the other Tolarenz recruits were already out on assignment. Vestgæta, I think. You're the only one we came for."

"Excellent," Askon said sarcastically.

"Just tryin' to warn you."

The group fanned out to their assigned lodging places to gather their belongings. As he strode through the camp, Askon noticed the smell of food. Several months spent at home, where meals were consistent, and consistently plentiful, only amplified his hunger. He crossed the camp to the smoldering remains of the central fire, searching for something to eat. After hailing one of the cooks, he was able to acquire a bit of bread and meat of questionable origin but interesting flavor. He sat on a bit of wood and proceeded to eat.

In the few moments he took to enjoy his meal, the camp bustled with activity. Within the first bites, Marten had found his place on the shoulder guard and was enjoying a similar breakfast. His beak clicked loudly as he worked through the hapless creature that had ventured too early from its home. Nearby, several young men were folding up canvas tents and tying them together in a sort of chain. Ropes were then wrapped around the entire bundle and knotted, allowing one animal to carry a number of shelters at once.

Throughout the camp, the grass and other plants had been trampled, not intentionally of course, but mashed and broken nonetheless. Wide spaces of bare earth between the patches of grass made for a terrific amount of dust. It rolled through the air and even in one breath, Askon could taste the stale dirt.

He stretched out and rocked back on his makeshift chair, thinking to himself how much Líana would have reveled in the dusty confusion of the camp. He imagined her running from tent to tent, scooping handfuls of ash and tossing them skyward, hoping to add to the choking mess. He mused on the thought of her tangled in the ropes that the men were using to bind the tents, and how she might have set a snare for an unsuspecting soldier.

"Líana!" he gasped aloud, drawing the gaze of the men at work nearby. In an instant he realized it. With the midnight surprise of his own fellows, and the rush to get on the move, he had forgotten to say goodbye to her. She was probably still hours from waking, but the prospect of going back was impossible. If the men had been upset at having to wait for him, they would be furious if he purposefully delayed them on account of his sister.

She would be crushed when she awoke later that morning. He promised himself that he would make it right upon his return, and even considered allowing her to attend one of his sessions with Caled.

The camp dwindled and the activity diminished. When he looked up, almost all evidence of their presence had gone. A matted patch of grass remained, and a few men tying the last of the tents. The dust still hung thick. He lifted his pack onto one shoulder, and with Marten on the other, walked toward the crowd. He heard a voice booming over the group.

"We ride east this morning," it sounded. "Keep with the line. We rest when we reach the river." Askon recognized the voice as that of Victor, his commanding officer since his very first military assignment. "The scouts have already left. We will follow in a few minutes' time. Be ready."

Though the border fort Austgæta was due east of Tolarenz, Askon guessed that they would first head south. Outside of the protective ring of mountains, the little river that flowed through the valley swelled with runoff from the outlying hills. A long march would bring them to a bridge that the soldiers would have to cross before making the climb to the plateau where Austgæta lay. Askon groaned at the thought of carrying his pack such a long way.

Then, out of the settling dust, the image of a man appeared. He was leading two horses. It was a relief, in more ways than one, to see that they wouldn't be walking. First, it would have lengthened the journey greatly, and second, it would have made for a much diminished store of energy for the fighting when they reached their destination.

"I had hoped you would come through again, John," Askon said, tightening a bootlace.

"Aye, but the whole lot of us are ridin' this time," John replied. "There's no need to thank me. He'd have been waitin' for you without my help."

"Well, needed or not, thanks for leading him over here."

The light of day was fully upon them now, the sun climbing from the edge of the mountains upward to the top of the sky. Thick clouds floated lazily along the ridges, though no threat of rain lay in their pure whiteness. Askon tied his pack to the horse. The beast snorted loudly, and Askon reached up, patting it on the neck. With a shake of its head, the horse's dark mane flopped from one side to the other. It stomped one foot impatiently as Askon vaulted into the saddle.

"Show off," said John, who had clumsily mounted his own horse. The two spurred their animals and headed south toward the larger group.

The ride was nothing if not painfully boring for everyone. The drone of hooves on the earth lulled them until a watchful eye could catch many nodding in the saddle. Askon saw one soldier fall completely from his horse. Luckily for him, the regiment had spread across a wide area, and he was spared from being trampled. And so Askon's immediate party gained a new member.

They halted, reigned up to help, and John rode ahead to retrieve the rider's masterless beast.

Once the young man had recovered, they found him to be a good companion. His name was Thomas and he was on his first assignment as a soldier. He claimed to be an accomplished rider, though Askon and his fellows noticed several mistakes and shortcomings in his technique. But their critical eyes were put to excellent use, as they found that the boy learned quickly and listened well.

The ride continued southward as the sun climbed higher. The light cloud-cover that had sheltered them in the morning had begun to dissipate, and though it was not yet noon, already the day seemed long and arduous. But at least for now, they had the river. Later on, the ride would take them away from the cool water and into the dry grassland that lay between the small tributary and the great river Estelle.

When the shadows of horse and rider had diminished to nothing, and the sun bore down angrily on the travelers, Askon and the accompanying soldiers sighted the bridge in the distance. It was a simple wooden structure, strong enough to support several horses and their riders.

After an hour's wait, mostly spent swatting flies or other bothersome insects, Askon's group crossed the bridge. All along its length, evidence of the regiment was left behind. Dirt and mud had smeared and mixed together to create a paste that caked and solidified in the sun. The boards had splintered at the corners, and deep horseshoe imprints dented the softened planks.

Askon took a last look back toward Tolarenz, and though the town had long been out of sight, he could still see the tips of the surrounding mountains in the haze at the edge of the sky. He turned to face his empty leather shoulder guard and wondered whether his companion was taking a last look as well from somewhere high above.

CHAPTER FOUR

On the March

On the other side of the bridge, the closeness was uncomfortable, and the flies found them again. Some of the younger soldiers held the horses in check. Thomas, being of the lowest rank in Askon's group, was given this task while the others collected river water for the journey across the dry plain. He performed admirably, leading the horses a short distance downstream to a wide space of grass that came directly to the water's edge. Here, the horses and their overseers drank and rested until the group at large was ready to proceed.

After the span of an hour, the company was ready to move. Askon and his friends had already found Thomas, remounted, and ridden ahead to find Victor. The horses meandered through the grass, their riders allowing them a few easy moments before Victor's voice echoed over the gathering troops.

"Bring it up together," he shouted. "Our path leads east, and don't expect to find water on this leg. It's straight across the plain this afternoon."

Askon turned to Thomas. "If you haven't filled your waterskins yet, do it now. You won't want to be caught without them later."

Thomas nodded in the affirmative while Victor's words poured over the crowd.

"Don't press the horses, but don't lag behind. We're still short on time," he boomed. Then, turning from the group, he spurred his horse forward. Askon and company did the same.

By now, the sun had moved past its highest point, yet the hottest was still to come. Runnels of sweat formed, and the river seemed to call them back, begging them to stay. The plains grass kept the dust down. For that they were grateful. The heat was enough without the choking haze that hung over the morning's encampment.

They were a dark company to be sure. Atop each animal, a black cloak flowed, King Codard's stag emblem shimmering blue in the center. Though the cloaks protected their skin from the direct glare of the sun, the heavy black cloth did little to deflect the heat. Before long, every man in the regiment was miserable. They became lazy in their riding and again began to sway in the saddle. But this time it wasn't for lack of sleep, instead the smothering cloaks brought them to a swoon.

One by one the whole company shed the cloaks and their riding equipment was revealed. Each man was equipped with a leather cuirass (the blue stag emblem at the chest), a short or long sword determined by preference, and a medium range bow with several arrows. For most, this armament was sufficient, but those of higher station or wealth often provided their own arms.

Askon carried the sword that his father had given him on his eighteenth birthday. It was of the absolute highest quality, forged and crafted by his friend Roland, the Tolarenz smith. The metal was of slightly differing alloy to those of the king's soldiers, much more difficult to produce, but lighter and more flexible. It had an intricately wrought handle and pommel similar to the baskets in Roland's garden and a comfortable grip that had been freshly wrapped prior to Askon's departure. It was currently bound at the left side of his mount, secure, yet loose enough to pull free easily if they were surprised.

The horses plodded along with their burdens, as eager as their riders to be rid of the glaring sun. Their heads swayed from side to side, seeking a bit of cool grass, and often their masters allowed the indulgence. A deep lull settled on the company, and the men drifted into daydream. None were immune, Askon included. He relaxed and allowed images of the town hall in Tolarenz to flow through his mind, structured only by the rhythmic hoofbeats and rocking motion of the saddle.

The company did have one observer, and the image was comic to some degree: a hundred soldiers totally unaware and lost in reverie. If enemies had somehow been able to cover themselves in the low grasses of the plain, the entire group was likely to be overwhelmed. They looked like dolls, ragged and lopsided, bobbing along. Having seen enough, the watcher plunged upon them, fully intending to cause a stir. He streaked down from an unfathomable height and gained nearly enough momentum to knock a rider from the saddle. The descent was silent, and accomplished his goal; Marten landed abruptly on Askon's shoulder, nearly toppling him to the ground.

"Marten," Askon exclaimed. He glared at the bird.

Marten happily plucked through the feathers at his breast, then shook himself, a puff of dust and plumage filling the air around him. He raised his head and stared back at his master for a moment before turning to survey the rest of the riders from his new vantage point. Thomas, who had witnessed the whole scene, spurred his horse to a trot until he and Askon rode side by side.

"That is an amazing bird you have there sir," he said.

"Thank you," Askon replied.

"There is one thing that confuses me though. Well, I guess it's a number of small things really," said Thomas nervously.

"Ask away."

"I've known people skilled in falconry, but I've never seen such a bird as yours. He has no jesses, wears no hood, and I've seen no lure anywhere. It's astonishing that he will even return to you at all."

Askon began to form a reply; the answer was complex and to a certain extent, inexplicable. But the conversation would have to wait. While Thomas had hurried to catch up, another group had been lagging, and both Askon and Thomas had overtaken them. The three men stayed close together, whispering. At this question, the man in the center spoke up.

"Aye, they hook 'em in with magic, they do. Potions what got made of boiled fingers and the like. Makes 'em do whatever they say, it does." The man sneered at Askon. One crooked tooth protruded from the grin, swelling his lower lip. "It's unnatural."

"Excuse me?" said Thomas, thoroughly confused.

"The half-breeds, you know, the long-ears."

No response.

"Ain't that one of our new recruits?" asked the shorter of the two, an obvious subordinate.

"Aye, he's the one who can't sit a horse." The three shared a derisive laugh. "Get back in line with the others, boy. I won't have one o' my men gettin' twisted up in no witchcraft."

Thomas's shoulders sagged, and he spurred the horse ahead. One of the three reached out and slapped him across the face. "Sit up straight," he ordered.

"Likely he's drugged him the same's his bird. Seen a lot of men die for those of his kind. Mind control and magic it is."

Askon smoldered under the heat of the sun and the words of the man whose fellows either laughed or gasped sarcastically as he spoke. And though Askon's anger rose quickly, he noticed the insignia that the man in the center bore. It was the same as his own, those worn by commanders, only with an additional bar signifying the man's higher station.

John urged his horse forward. "Hey!" he shouted. "Aren't you Commander Landon?"

The man at the center turned to face him. "Aye. What's it to you anyway?"

John shrugged. "I got orders from Victor to send some o' the recruits to the lower officers like this one here." He indicated Askon. "I figure he could take another half-dozen if you got 'em."

Commander Landon shook his head. "No. Them others are well-trained already. I ain't seen one fall off his horse yet." He hesitated. "But this one's probably already under the spell o' that pointy-eared bastard. Might as well take him. He'll only slow us down anyway."

John grunted a response and waved ahead to Thomas. It was all a lie, Askon knew, but a clever one, and one that the other commander would be unlikely to pursue. Recruits joined companies on nearly every assignment, often shifting from one officer's command to the next, and every one required training, additional work that a good number of officers would rather avoid. Many such recruits had come and gone from Askon's own ranks; some on orders, others because they couldn't stand taking orders from a half-elf.

"And be careful fallin' in with one such as that," Landon called as he and his men fell further back. "I hear they can get pretty cozy with the farm-boy newcomers if they take a likin' to 'em."

The three laughed amongst themselves again, and Askon spurred his horse, attempting to put distance between them. John hurried to catch up.

"Don't listen to 'em, Askon, you know their type, not worth the time or effort."

"You would think that they would eventually tire of comments like that." Askon looked over his shoulder. The other men were still laughing. "It makes me wonder if they'll ever accept Tolarenz and its people."

"That lot? Not a chance, if I had to hazard a guess. But there's plenty who will, and already a good many who do."

Askon wished that John was right, but in truth, most of the leaders regarded Tolarenz as a haven for outsiders at best. Askon was a special case because of his involvement in rescuing King Codard's son, Edward. And often, even that wasn't enough.

Thomas's horse jogged up beside them. "Sir," Thomas began. "I'm a bit confused. What was he referring to?"

"He's half-elf. Can't you see that?" John said abruptly.

"N—no, I can't," stammered Thomas. "I grew up in the farm country. I can't say I've ever met someone like that."

"You have now," said Askon.

"Use your brain, man. How do ya think he gets his bird to do what he wants?"

"So all that about boiling fingers is true?"

"Oh you're hopeless." John threw his hands in the air. Thomas, as confused as ever, looked first to John and then to Askon.

"It's not magic," Askon said. "And there are no boiled fingers involved." He looked at Marten, who was still perched on his shoulder. "It's simple really. I ask him and he responds. We understand each other. If I ask a favor, it is expected to be repaid, and so it is in his turn as well."

Thomas tipped in the saddle, leaning toward Marten. "But these creatures are wild, predatory animals. No one in hundreds of years of falconry has ever trained one like a dog. That must be a one-in-a-million bird."

"He is called Marten," Askon replied, "and he is not unique. It's an elvish tradition that I've only seen practiced by one falconer. His name is Halan, and he lives in Tolarenz."

"There exists a falconer who can train without hoods, jesses, or lures?" Thomas asked, eyes wide. "That's incredible!"

John, having heard many similar conversations before, sighed and fell back a few paces. The boy was curious. They were always curious at first, but more often than not, that curiosity turned to misunderstanding and then suspicion.

Askon gave him a chance anyway. "It's not quite *that* simple," he said. "The early process is still similar to the falconry that your family practices. It isn't until later that the equipment is discarded and the free stage begins."

"So, are you saying that I could learn this technique and bring my own birds to the…free stage?" Thomas examined Marten, drawing ever closer until it seemed he would topple off his horse again.

"I'm not sure," Askon said. Though he was fairly certain that such a feat would not be possible.

Thomas slumped back into the saddle, a pensive furrow crossing his brow. A few moments passed, and the two rode in silence, but Askon, seeing the change, instilled some hope back into his listener.

"Perhaps some day I'll introduce the two of you. It wouldn't hurt for you to try to learn," he said.

Thomas's face brightened immediately. "Thank you. I would enjoy that."

The talk of falconry went on, and by the time Askon had answered Thomas's final question, much of the day had passed. There was a long discussion about the appropriate bird for the appropriate rank of citizen, and a heated debate on whether eagles were considered proper falcons. Throughout the conversation, Thomas proved a great sponge, taking in every bit of wisdom that Askon would offer him, though they always returned to the manner in which Askon could command Marten. Was it a language? No. Did Askon have to be taught to command him? No. Did the humans of Tolarenz have falcons like Marten? Yes. And so on.

When the topic had been exhausted, there came a deep rumble. Perhaps, Askon thought, the oncoming hoofbeats of a large herd. It was a heavy vibration that rose up from the ground and saturated the air. He found soon enough that he was, in fact, mistaken. It was no oncoming herd, rather the sound of the great river droning away to the south. They crested a small rise in the plain and beheld the river Estelle.

The river was far too wide and deep to be forded by any horse, and too strong and rocky to be crossed by boat. Its gray foam crashed against the banks, and fierce stones rose from the open water. The roar deepened. At first they assumed that it was simply the sound of the river, but after edging ever nearer, this seemed impossible.

Some way to the north, the plain climbed steeply, and a stand of thick trees covered both banks of the river. Sparkling in the dazzling light that filtered green through the trees was an immense waterfall. Hundreds of feet it fell, past a sheer rock face to the plain below. There had been attempts, it appeared, to climb the cliffside, but the best effort was a narrow pathway that ventured only a quarter of the distance. In one place, the path crossed the span where an ancient stone bridge arched over the thundering pool. On the other side, the path wound behind the fall and did not continue beyond; the face became almost completely vertical.

The soldiers gathered at the foot of the cliff, a sense of wonder pervading the group. There was no escaping it. One was forced to succumb to the waterfall's presence and constant reverberations. Victor appeared on the bridge—the only place where the entire company would have been able to see him. He motioned to them, conveying that they were to rest, eat, and replenish their stores of water.

Most of the men had now forgotten the morning's heat, but the experienced travelers among them knew that the worst was still ahead. The next day would afford no water between the great falls and Austgæta. The company would be forced to skirt the sheer face of the plateau before them, sidling around it until they reached the gentler side. They would then climb the slope under the midday heat and ride the rest of the day before reaching the outpost at the borderlands.

Though the mist at first was a nuisance, causing Askon's clothes to cling and his hair to dampen, he was soon overcome. And with no spontaneous noises to disturb him, he slept peacefully at the foot of the droning falls. A similar process repeated throughout the camp. With no ability to communicate due to the rushing water, none lay awake, and the night's darkness surrounded them.

In the morning the group woke at first light. Victor and a few others were up and strolling about the camp, kicking and shaking the still sleeping men; it was like trying to raise the dead. The relatively slow pace of the previous day was obviously not to be repeated. Tents were wrapped again in the chain-link fashion. Breakfasts were hastily prepared, though none of them hot. This time there was no dust, but the mist was always present, hanging heavily, wetly.

Askon woke John first, who reveled in finding creative ways with which to awaken his friends. He went about his work, this time choosing panfuls of icy cold water while Askon readied the horses. Thomas and the others, spluttering and soaking from John's practical jokes, prepared to move out of the area, their voices still useless against the thunder of the falls. Askon waved them onward.

Slowly, the roar died away and the company felt the press of sunlight from the east. The damp of the previous night lifted, and swirling fingers of steam rose from the mounted forms. All along their right side were the mountains, upon whose plateau the great river flowed before crashing down into the grove of trees. The mountains started gradually, and small patches of trees and brush grew in the runoff of the rolling foothills. The regiment rode at the very base of these trees, hoping to find shade at their edges.

Riding from the waterfall to their final destination was a much more difficult chore than from Tolarenz to the fall. The pace was greater, and though the heat of the sun was less direct, the humidity was inescapable. To reach Austgæta they would have to follow the hills to a more gradual slope that the horses could climb. And so the journey grew longer. On this day there would be no breaks, stops, or delays.

"Oh no, not at this rate we won't," John was saying, as the group crested a small rise. "We've got the whole flatland at the top to cross."

"Tomorrow maybe," said another man.

"Companies make this journey often," corrected Askon. "If Victor aims to reach Austgæta by sundown, he'll reach it."

"That's all well and good Askon, but what about the rest of us?" John quipped. Muffled laughter rippled through the group.

"Well, I intend to keep pace, as will anyone under my command."

Thomas bounced along beside them, still looking uncomfortable in the saddle. "You also mentioned that the army has traveled this way before," he said. "Have you been to this outpost?"

"No," Askon said. More muffled laughter ran through the group. "I *have* been to the borderlands several times, at varying outposts, but never this one."

They rode on, and slowly the laughter died away. Thomas leaned closer. "I overheard some of the other officers discussing your time at one of those outposts. The one in the northwest."

"Vestgæta," said Askon. He looked out over the sun-gold fields into the west.

"Yes, that's it," said Thomas with some excitement. "They were saying that you rescued the king's son in a battle there."

"I did only what was required of me," said Askon humbly.

"Rubbish!" exclaimed John. "You'd make it out like somebody gave you the order, Askon." He looked to Thomas and slapped him on the back. "I'll tell you how it all went.

"It was a good while back, five years probably, and we'd all been marched over to Vestgæta to burn out a Norill nest up there. There was a good sight worth of the enemy, and they were workin' their way down the mountains toward the outpost. They had set up camp a few miles north of us, and we hoped to keep an eye their comings and goings. That's where the king's boy, Edward, came in. His specialty is scout work and reconnaissance. The commanders sent him and some boys out, hopin' to find a place where we could set an ambush. They found one." John took a drink from his waterskin. He had an audience, and he knew it.

"Edward sent back one of his boys, givin' us the location. We got armed and ready, and followed his lead. Victor was leadin'— as per the usual—and Askon and I were among the regular infantry. Outfitted 'bout as we are today. Well, we climbed up to the spot—no horses that day—and we set about searchin' for Edward. Looked all around there for quite a while and finally landed on a stretch o' brush all trampled and broken. Seemed they'd found him and his boys out and hauled 'em off." John paused for effect. Thomas listened intently.

"So," John continued. "The first thought was to call the ambush off and move out back to camp. Victor was already makin' preparations when Askon comes up to him with a few of us. He tells Victor we got no choice but to go in for Edward. Rightly, I think, Victor shuts him up and tells him to fall in and get back to the outpost.

"See, what we didn't know was that the scouts had seen what we were up against. The full force was settled right down the hill. If we were discovered we'd have been overmatched. We were only a side force. The main group had stayed back.

"Now Askon's got some great qualities, don't get me wrong, but he's got an irrational streak. After Victor says no, Askon goes right back to the group of us and says we can go back if we like, but he's goin' in for Edward." John leaned back in the saddle and looked to Askon.

"You want to tell this part?" he asked.

"No," replied Askon. "You finish."

"Alright," said John. "I said that I'd rather be in our barracks than in theirs, so I went with the larger group. Askon, takes the scout, who didn't want to leave his commander behind, and goes straight into the camp at nightfall. He takes two guards by himself at the north end while the scout takes another two at the south. The whole lot o' the camp went piling out to the south end, which was struck first. Askon went in through the back and cut Edward loose. People say they took ten more of the enemy on their way out."

"People, when they tell stories like that, are almost always wrong," said Askon thinking back to the night five years earlier. There had been no other scout. John knew this as well as anyone, but the official story always included an assistant. The captains and other leaders could not believe that the rescue had been made by just one man, and a half-elf at that.

"At any rate," John said after the interruption, "they climbed straight out of there and made it back to the outpost before first light. I was taking bets already on whether Askon would come back, but I doubled my money when he brought Edward with him. Victor made him a commander on the spot—Askon, I mean—despite going against orders."

"What happened to the other man, the scout?" Thomas asked.

"I was told that the Norill overwhelmed him. He died at the south gate to the enemy camp," said Askon quietly. His eyes still gazed to the west; he turned away abruptly, spurring his horse ahead.

"He never did feel right about it all," said John after a moment, but it wasn't the loss of a man in the field that troubled Askon. It was the lie.

They rode on for some time, Askon ahead of them, now and then looking back to the west. The groves of trees passed by, the company moving in and out of the shade.

"Where is Edward now?" Thomas asked.

"Well, from what I hear, and this is just what I hear," John said, "the king's army has two units out at present. One's us and we're the larger. The other is, according to the rumors, a secret mission led by Edward. All I know is that they were sent out from King's City at about the time I left. A few've been sayin' that it's some kind of artifact they're after. I don't know if I believe it myself. The king's got his hands full at the borderlands, and he refuses to move much of the army away from the city. Always seemed like a waste to me. Gotta be thousands of 'em sittin' there waiting for orders."

"That does seem like a waste," said Thomas.

Though he had ridden ahead to distance himself from the memories of Vestgæta, Askon overheard every word that passed between Thomas and John. Marten was at his side again, tilting his head curiously at the swaying grass and shifting lightly from foot to foot. Askon considered Edward's pursuit. An artifact of some kind, they had said. It was only two days earlier that Askon and Caled had discussed Alora's Tear and the possibility of its existence. If Edward were to find it and hand it over to King Codard, what would that mean for Tolarenz? Askon tried to imagine what the king might otherwise be looking for, but there was no alternative.

The day passed along, and again the cloaks were dropped in an effort to relieve the heat. By noon, the company had rounded the mountains and climbed the pass to the top of the plateau where billowing white clouds passed across the blazing sun. Far to the west—near Tolarenz by Askon's estimation—the clouds darkened and a thin mist fell below.

The air on the plateau seemed cleaner and clearer than that of the plain. And though the flatland was itself a sort of plain, nearly everything about it was different from the terrain that they had traversed the day before. Flowers bloomed in pale pink and yellow, and thin stalked plants covered the ground, their purple blossoms crowding together at the ends of the stems. In some places these flowers stretched for acres along the path, on the company's left as far as they could see, and on the right all the way to the river.

Later in the evening, when the men had made contact with the water, they commented on its unrivaled purity. In one quick glance Askon could see the basin of solid rock that the water flowed along at the top of the plateau. No silt or sediment of any kind sullied the waters, just a pure clean stream running a gently winding course to plunge hundreds of feet into the clinging mist and encircling trees.

The sun sank slowly into the west, its glowing tendrils touching the rim of the northern horizon. There, illuminated against the coming blackness, stood the outpost: banners high in the breeze, its surface gray and sun-bleached, and behind it the slowly sloping mountain. The narrow poles that made up the outer walls and defenses were sharpened at the ends, giving the place the look of some toothy, ancient beast half-buried in the fine soil of the mountainside.

CHAPTER FIVE
A Cold Reception

Night birds called and squawked in the darkness. The horses snorted nervously under a sliver of pale moonlight. Just minutes after sunset the temperature dropped dramatically, leaving the men rubbing their arms for warmth. Voices carried clearly from the gates to the farthest reaches of the company; the leaders were discussing something with the keepers of Austgæta. At Askon's request, Thomas and John had remained behind. There they listened to the conversation as it drifted through the crisp night air.

Askon rode ahead and waited, reins in hand, mere feet from the entrance. The company's several other commanders were also present as Victor's voice boomed into the faces of the guardsmen who refused to allow the company passage through the gate.

"We were told to make haste to Austgæta by order of the king," he shouted. "What person of sound mind would hold out reinforcements?"

None of the guards moved, but one spoke in measured tones, almost as if he were bored by Victor's questions. "Our orders prevent us from allowing anyone through these gates after sunset."

"Do you expect us to make camp in the field tonight?" Victor roared. "If the danger is so great, we would be a perfect target out here."

"None are allowed to pass after nightfall," was the guard's response.

Askon bristled. He would not allow a glorified doorman to put his company in danger. "My men will not be forced to sleep, undefended, at the very doorstep of our assigned outpost." In the pale glow of the moon, his eyes glimmered defiance from beneath his hood.

Another rider moved forward, out of the row of commanders. "It's prob'ly your account what's makin' 'em bar our entry," said the horseman, and Askon recognized Landon, the commander who had warned Thomas about the elves. "I wouldn't trust a comp'ny harborin' no half-elves neither."

The guard at center perked up, stirred from his apathy. "How many half-elves are among your forces?" he asked suspiciously.

"Just the one," said Landon. "Lock him up for all I care, as long as we can pass." The guard made a slight movement in

Askon's direction. Instantly the long knife was unsheathed and flashing in the night.

"You'll do nothing of the sort," barked Victor. "And that will be enough out of you," he said to Landon.

What the three of them had failed to notice were the shadows appearing at intervals atop the wall. As many as fifteen bows were currently aimed directly at the company's leaders. Arrows knocked, strings taught, any false movement could be fatal. The guardsman, stoic as ever, peered at them through the dark, his eyes fixated on Askon's knife.

"We have authorization to kill any aggressive forces," he said frowning, first pointing up and to his right, then to the left, indicating the bowmen.

"Askon, that is enough. Put it away," said Victor cooly.

The knife slid back into the sheath and rested with a metallic click; then the bows lowered, and the whole area, men, grass, horses, mountain, even the air seemed to relax.

"I will no longer debate the issue with simple footmen," said Victor after a pause. "Alert someone of the appropriate rank immediately. Where is your general?" There was no compromise in his voice, only icy cold command and the frigid assumption of compliance. One of the guards broke and called to the men above.

"Find the general," he shouted. The lead guardsman glared at the display of weakness, threatening what would later be a severe punishment, but remained in his position at the gate.

An agonizing length of time passed, Victor coldly refusing further discourse, Askon seething at being held out, and the guardsmen waiting for any excuse to take action. The general finally appeared on the wall, flanked by two heavily armed archers.

"Declare your name and purpose," the grizzled man said.

"I am Victor of Reed, servant of King Codard, here on orders to reinforce the outpost at Austgæta." Victor had assumed a tone of general authority and strict formality. Every trace of his earlier irritation evaporated like the steam that puffed from the horses' noses. "These are my men."

The general peered down from the battlements, his narrow eyes mere specks of black in the night. He lifted a hand to his graying beard. "Reed. How does a man from a village so deep in the northern woods come to command a company?" He expected no answer, and Victor gave none. "No. The enemy is near," he said slowly. "We have been deceived by them to our great loss in the past." He paused, pulling at the beard again. "My earlier command must be upheld. These gates will not open until sunrise."

"That is an insult!" Askon shouted. "We will not be disrespected in this way, left to defend open ground in the night."

"Control your men, Victor of Reed, or an unsheltered night will be the least of your worries," growled the general. Victor shot a threatening glare at Askon who had taken a step forward.

"I said, enough, Askon," he said aloud. Then more quietly, "Accept it or you'll get us killed." Askon stepped back, vainly struggling to contain his rage. He lowered his head to conceal his face, and ground his teeth together while the general and Victor argued on.

After a number of additional exchanges, the outcome remained the same. Victor's forces, Askon and his men included, would remain outside the outpost until sunrise. The leaders returned to the larger group, preparing for the inevitable response. Askon was the first to reach his men; he delivered the instruction haltingly, trying to restrain his contradictory feelings. Thomas accepted the command immediately, while John railed against the decision. The others debated the general's judgement, often in animated fashion, but all eventually submitted and prepared a minimal camp for the night. A watch was set, and the men fell into fitful sleep amongst tufts of grass and cold stones.

Screams shot through the camp from all directions, and the sounds of clashing swords echoed across the frigid tundra. Askon was on his feet in an instant. The blurred haze of sleep lifted from his eyes, and he brought himself back to the ground. The company had been arranged in a square pattern across the open field. Of the watchmen, who had been set four-to-a-corner, none remained alive. Their bodies lay limply, pierced by the enemy's thin black arrows.

Torches flickered to life throughout the camp, and the wavering light illuminated a grisly scene. A significant number of the company's men had been killed even before they could rise, especially those to the south where the enemy had struck hardest. Askon's men—who made up the northwest corner of the camp—

had remained relatively safe. He glanced to the wall of the outpost and saw Austgæta's archers, their hands gliding swiftly from quiver to string in a steady loop. Their bowshots contained the threat at the northern corners, but the south was out of reach.

At the corner opposite Askon, the torchbearers had been struck down, and the flames had taken to the grasses on the plain. They burned slowly in the damp night, filling the battlefield with thick smoke that affected enemy as much as ally. The fighting drifted away from the choking smolder. It was here that the casualties were the greatest.

John woke any who remained sleeping, and Askon's men formed a loose collection behind their leader. He motioned John to take one group to the west while he led the other into the smoke. Thomas, armed yet shaking with fear, followed Askon. The two parties separated and moved quickly through the carnage.

Victor had massed a large formation to directly assault the main threat in the southwest. His men fought valiantly, though they knew not the number of their enemies nor how many still lurked in the darkness. Their forced encampment had indeed made them an easy target. They were only lightly armored and some unarmed. But in spite of the surprise, Victor's forces slowly drove the enemy farther south.

The Norill fought back like animals, and were dressed similarly. They lumbered across the battlefield in furs or armor made of bleached bones and the skulls of various creatures. As they were driven closer together, they seemed to grow in strength, and soon

Victor's men began falling to their crude weapons. Victor called a retreat, and the press of battle moved back toward Austgæta's wall.

The fighting continued in a form of stalemate, with the enemy pushing Victor's forces nearer and nearer the smoke. Great lines of Norill crashed into Victor's defenses, scattering them. And just as the men regrouped and engaged the line, a second lighter Norill force would rush in to support, killing swiftly and mercilessly, often stabbing men in the back or isolating a soldier three to one. The enemy lines then fell back, and the process repeated. Little by little, Victor's forces either died or retreated, ever moving eastward toward the fire.

As the stooping, snarling, assemblage of bones and animal skins set their armor and tightened the leather straps that tied their weapons to gnarled arms, a call issued from the west. It was echoed in the smoke to the east and Askon's men crashed into the flanks of the enemy. Though their armor was gruesome and heavy in the front, it left their backs unprotected. Between the hammer and anvil of Askon and John, the Norill force shattered. Those that did not fall were exposed to Victor's remaining forces in the north.

Askon's sword flashed brilliantly through the dim light, killing at will until a heavily armed brute knocked his sword to the ground. He took a second blow and fell to his stomach where he rolled quickly out of reach.

Crouching there, he waited for the next stroke to fall. And just before the massive weapon struck the ground, he leapt forward and plunged the hunting knife into an opening between the bone plates near the base of the creature's neck. The Norill flailed wildly as Askon's momentum carried him back across to where his sword lay. The next brutal stroke missed by a wide margin and the arm continued to the earth, severed clean by Askon's recovered sword. The left hand swung in vain while the stump of the other poured gouts of blood down the creature's side. Askon deftly avoided the wild attacks, until the creature stepped forward with a furious roar. Askon buried his sword in its great chest. His opponent fell heavily, again wrenching the sword from his hand.

He yanked his weapons free of the Norill corpse and surveyed the ongoing battle. To his right, John was finishing off another of the heavily armed creatures. Behind him, Victor's forces had gained the advantage. The men were allowing the lines to pass and then focusing directly on the lightly armored support. With the aggressors dead, the slow, clumsy line members were easily isolated. Askon peered through the smoke and found Thomas parrying and defending erratically, as one of the light units slashed at him with a short-sword and crude hatchet.

Before Askon could reach him, the tide began to turn. Thomas deflected a violent stroke of the axe and sent the creature spinning off balance. He moved forward and struck again and again at the fallen enemy. He was nearly at a victory when a thrust of his sword went wide, and the creature's axe landed broadside in his ribs. Thomas crashed to the ground. The Norill climbed to its feet, and two more appeared out of the smoke. Askon, by now engaged again in combat, struggled toward his friend. The creatures surrounded Thomas, the original attacker still swinging wildly as Thomas continued to fall back. With a desperate sword stroke, Askon parried his opponent's weapon and spun quickly, sinking the knife deep into its side. He pulled hard on the handle and opened a gash across the Norill's midsection. Its life spilled from the opening in tangled lumps, and Askon left it there to die. He sprinted to Thomas's aid.

The new arrivals drove Thomas back into the third Norill over and over again. They were toying with him. Askon felt the anger and adrenaline rise as he burst through the ring. The largest of the three fell instantly, its sparse armor split with a sharp *crack* and a soft squelch under Askon's stroke. Rolling with the first blow, Askon sprang toward his next target. The creature was prepared, and met him with resistance. It parried the first attack and countered, but Askon caught the arm and twisted away. The pommel of Askon's sword splintered the bone helmet, and the creature fell to its knees. The second pommel strike smashed through the fragile bones of its face. It toppled over backwards and twitched weakly in the grass.

Meanwhile, Thomas continued his struggle, finally catching a wayward sword slash with his own. He thrust it to the side, sending his attacker to the ground with its back fully exposed. He pushed with all his weight on the hilt of the sword, and the point sank into the squirming body.

All around them, the battle was drawing to a close. Victor's forces had systematically eliminated the light offensive units, and what was left of the larger creatures either fled or died on the field. A light was glowing in the east, the sun and accompanying morning approached. Men smothered fires, and the remaining smoke drifted briskly across the plain.

As the last remnants of the enemy fell, Askon and his men moved through the piled bodies, checking for survivors. There were few, but those who still clung to life were taken onto the shoulders of the able and carried to the gate. Victor, red-faced and angry, the veins in his neck pulsing with the last surge of battle, shouted up to the archers. "Open the gates! We have fought and died to prove ourselves. We must tend to the wounded."

The towering doors swung outward slowly, their weight heavy on creaking hinges. When they had opened to a width of four men, the motion ceased, and the company passed inside the walls. Some men limped awkwardly, while others had to be carried on shoulders, or at worst, on wide wooden boards brought from within.

There was an initial rush toward the gates, but others remained outside or returned for their belongings and their horses. Askon and his men were among the last of the company to enter, laden with supplies that had not yet been recovered. John had suffered several blunt wounds that were already beginning to bruise, but he walked upright and made jokes at the expense of their fallen opposition. Thomas was exhilarated. How close he had come to the end of his life, he had yet to realize, but Askon allowed him to relish the victory. The horses stamped and snorted, anxious after the surprise in the night. Marten dove through the air to land safely at Askon's shoulder. He wondered where the bird had been when the enemy emerged from the darkness. The sun broke free of the mountains, and Askon entered Austgæta.

CHAPTER SIX

Austgæta

"Vile creatures! Worthy only of extermination." It was the general's turn to show his anger now. "Time and again they surprise us, even when we think we are prepared for them." He spat into the dirt at his feet, his thick, curling beard catching most of it.

"Indeed the Norill are crafty, but this is a fact that we've known for many years. Shutting us out only served to increase our losses." Victor's voice was calm and slow, without a trace of his earlier anger.

"We knew they were coming, Victor of Reed. Your company could very well have been a trap," the general said. "Perhaps you've been on leave for too long. Austgæta is out of the way, and we are wary. We take care of our own." He looked across the outpost to a low tent where soldiers were receiving medical attention. An anguished cry tore through the tent flap, then faltered and fell silent. "Your men have suffered," he said with a heavy sigh.

Askon burst forward, knocking Victor off balance. "Those who are dead do not suffer," he said, staring defiantly into the general's face. "And what compensation can you offer for your incompetence?"

"I can offer you a place in confinement if you do not show the proper respect," snarled the general, instantly bristling. "This man has overstepped before, Victor. Do you make a habit of surrendering command to inferior officers?"

"I do not, General," Victor replied. "But my commanders lead men of their own, and I expect them to protect those men." He grasped Askon's cloak, pulling him back until the two were at an even position.

"See that they address you with their grievances, not me," said the general. "Do not forget, you are all my men now. Your commanders are dismissed."

Victor waved Askon and the other officers away with a flick of one hand, while the other pinched his temples. In a swirl of green and great puffs of dust, Askon left them behind. The general and Victor ignored him, lost in their animated discussion of the battle. Their voices quickly faded in the clamor of the outpost.

As he walked across the open area which the local soldiers called the yard, he saw essentially a functioning village in miniature. At the southeast corner, sheep and goats bayed in anticipation of the morning meal. Their pen was cramped; in

Tolarenz only half as many animals would have been kept in one of similar size.

The same mindset prevailed throughout the yard. Smiths worked side by side with only enough room to swing from forge to anvil between them; a constant pinging and rush of heat emanated from their corner. In another area, a vegetable garden was planted in rows so narrow that no grown man could pass between them without disturbing the stalks. The horses were tied along an open space near the wall, and a stable master cycled through the animals, feeding and grooming them so that they were always in shape for travel or battle. Beyond the wall on the northern side, a large plot of grain grew. It was the only food source not inside the walls. If the Norill were to attempt an attack on this small plot of land, they would have bowmen to deal with, that is, if they weren't already victims of the traps set in the surrounding trees.

Unlike the camp outside of Tolarenz, the dust in Austgæta was bearable. For this, Askon felt grateful as he continued across the yard. John and Thomas sorted their provisions, engaged in a debate of some sort, when Askon finally reached them. They sat opposite each other on pieces of firewood that wobbled as they talked, giving Askon the impression that they were constantly trying to balance their makeshift chairs and win the argument at the same time.

"They're dogs!" John said rocking to his left. "Not a bit of man in there, I can tell you that."

"But why then, do they walk upright as we do?" Thomas asked.

"A bear can walk on two legs, can't it? You don't have lunch with him, do you?"

"Well, if not that, then explain this." Thomas produced a piece of the bone armor that the heavier units wore. On its bleached white face, scrawlings ran vertically and horizontally across the plate.

"What did you bring that in here for!" John shouted, slapping the plate away. It clattered across the dirt and matted grass, stopping at Askon's feet.

"They look like runes of some kind to me," Askon said, turning the plate in his hand.

"Oh you would side with him Askon," John muttered. "You'll be wantin' a tea party next, I suppose."

"What are you two even talking about?"

"The boy here thinks the Norill might just want to discuss politics and lore with us," John laughed. "Apparently they're just tryin' to give us a culture lesson by slaughtering men in the night!"

"I didn't say that," Thomas mumbled under his breath. He kicked a tuft of grass, nearly toppling from his firewood perch.

"What did you say then?" asked Askon. "I've had some experience with the Norill, and I think I can articulate my position better than John might."

"Now I'm too stupid to tell the boy about a lot o' monsters we've been fightin' for years? Makes sense to me that we should find their capital and burn it straight out. Leave nothin' whatever behind us 'cept their bodies. They'd do no better to us if they got the chance." John stood and stormed away.

Askon watched him go. "He'll cool off, and I have to say that I agree with him on most of those points. I've seen things from the Norill that would freeze the blood in your veins. Last night's battle was a scuffle. You did well. But you will see worse before your time in this company is finished."

"Perhaps," Thomas said. "What I can't let go of is that I think they are men, just as you and I are. The one I killed, his eyes stared back, hateful, fearful. I wondered if my eyes would have looked the same had you not come along." He glanced cautiously from side to side, expecting a reaction similar to John's. "You, of all people should understand."

Askon moved closer, his eyes gleaming. "You would do well to never compare the elves to the Norill again," he said. "My people are misunderstood, but you saw what those creatures are capable of. You saw the skulls, and the skins. Do you think those are all from animals of the forest?" Askon grabbed the bone plate and threw it against the wall; it splintered at a weakened seam, before falling to the ground. "Their leaders wear the bones of our dead."

Askon left Thomas and followed John toward the horses. His cloak rippled with each step. Thomas, face pale, eyes downcast, said nothing. When Askon had put some distance between them, he stared across the yard at a wooden cage. Inside prisoners captured the night before and in battles previous. Behind the thick bars, two large Norill crouched in a thin space of shade. Others were scattered at various intervals, but one stood at the gate. It was staring back. The thin, starved body was only barely able to stand, but the eyes—black and cold—bored into

Askon's. He shaded his face with his hood and turned from the creature. John thrashed angrily through the supplies, and Askon could feel the Norill's eyes on his back.

"John," he said, shaking off the feeling. "Why don't you leave that. Thomas will finish up here. Come on." He motioned to a narrow wooden staircase that led to the guard posts atop the western wall.

"Probably take the lot to the prisoners as presents, won't he?" asked John, as he glared at Thomas.

"He's just trying to understand them," said Askon calmly.

"Oh, I understand them all right. Boy should listen is all I'm sayin'."

"Just leave it for now," Askon continued. "And please stop calling him 'boy.' What are you? Five years older than him?"

"It's a long five, by my count."

"Even so, it doesn't help the situation."

Askon motioned to Thomas and then to the bags and equipment. The young man understood immediately and proceeded to move and organize the items. Askon and John climbed the stairs single file, the boards creaking as they walked. At the top stood a low wooden parapet of about three feet. The sharpened ends of the individual poles that made up the wall gleamed like splintered bones. Askon leaned against one and stared into the west. John rested against a particularly sharp post. The clamor of Austgæta continued below; forges hissed, anvils pinged, and from time to time one of the prisoners would burst out in wild noises, banging at the bars of the cage.

Askon gazed across the open plateau. He could see the gentle slope that they had climbed far off in the haze of distance; to the north, thick trees brooded in the shadows at the foot of the mountain. On the plateau, flowers and plants of all kinds flourished, the dew on each petal sparkling in the morning light. Marten decided to join them, balancing on a spike along the wall. To the west, the plateau dropped steeply to the plains below where many miles off lay Norogæta, and farther yet, the little green valley of Tolarenz.

Askon waved off two men stationed at the watch, giving them leave for a short break. He and John stood in silence for some time, enjoying the morning air. At length, Askon spoke.

"Perishia," he said. "You know they say that this plateau is Perishia."

John looked incredulous. "What, like the island from the stories?"

"I was thinking of one story specifically," said Askon. "Before I left Tolarenz, Lord Caled suggested that Alora and Heraphus may have been real, and the Tear as well."

"Ha!" John laughed, standing up straight and stretching. "We'd be lucky to find that, wouldn't we? I bet it'd sell pretty steep, if you could find a buyer."

"Probably," Askon answered offhandedly. "If it was real though, do you think that it might be on this plateau somewhere?"

"The only things up here besides grass, flowers, and the mountain are this outpost, and that festering hole of a Norill colony up north." He spat disgustedly over the edge of the wall. "Hopefully we can look there one day when we burn the rats' nest to the ground."

"I doubt we would find it there," said Askon, still staring into the west.

"Bein' rid of that menace at any rate, would be good enough," said John.

"I think we can agree on that."

The two stood quietly for a while. A breeze agitated the whole of the field into a ripple like the surface of a vast green lake. Marten circled over them, watching for any additional movement, but the wind on the brush made for difficult hunting.

Behind them, the outpost continued its operations. Thomas had finished organizing their equipment and now wandered through the yard, talking to the various soldiers who made Austgæta their permanent home. Before long, the two guardsmen returned with bread and water. The short time away from their post had visibly raised their spirits, and they thanked Askon and John heartily. On the way down, Askon's eyes met those of the Norill prisoner once again.

"I'll talk to you later John," he said. "Please try to go a little easier on Thomas."

"I will," John said with a laugh. "But only so long as he doesn't start arguin' the enemy's cause again."

John started toward the walled area that served as a barracks for the new arrivals. Askon continued across the yard, an irresistible force pulling him toward the Norill prisoners. Approaching the wooden bars, he saw that the staring prisoner had retreated to the rear of the cell. It was crouched, arms wrapped around its knees, now staring at the dusty floor of the cage. Long stringy hair dangled from its head and dragged on the ground.

Askon crouched warily, putting himself at the same level. He tilted his head slightly, and lowered it, trying to get a better view of the creature's face. As he did, the strands of hair lifted like tiny snares, and the fierce eyes locked to Askon's. How long he stared into those eyes, Askon could not tell. Something in that deep darkness reminded him of home, where his mother's eyes would pierce to the heart, but these were a twisted parody of that memory. They were black as the night sky, a void, not seeing into one's soul, rather devouring it. Askon could feel fear creeping in, and the sky seemed to darken. He found himself edging closer to the bars, but in his mind he resisted, pulling away from the gaze like a frightened child.

In an instant the creature had his arm. The grip was crushing, and seemed to slice through the skin of his wrist. Askon twisted, but the cold gray fingers were latched into place. The darkness continued to grow and a chill crawled up Askon's spine. All the while, the eyes smoldered, holding Askon fast with even more strength than the hand.

"Where is stone-of-mountain?" a voice screeched. It was raspy and cold, and Askon felt as though it would echo throughout the camp.

Askon's voice shook. "Stone of the mountain?"

"Where is!" the voice screamed. Askon fell to one knee. It was like fire in his brain.

"I don't know," he whimpered. The darkness sank to pure black and Askon was alone, writhing on the ground, but the grip persisted.

"We will not stop. More will come." Now the voice was huge, pressing down like a boulder, grinding Askon into the dust. "Tell where is stone-of-mountain!" it repeated, only much louder and with such force that it pushed all the air out of Askon's lungs.

"No more," he choked. Another hand grasped his shoulder, and with all the strength Askon could muster, he twisted his body and wrenched himself free, instantly drawing the knife sheathed at his side.

"Let me go!" he shouted.

Sunlight burst through the shadow and Askon was standing face-to-face with one of the local soldiers, knife drawn. The man raised both hands and stepped back.

"Hey," he said uneasily, retreating a bit further. "You should keep away from the prisoners. They're dangerous. Though it seems you are, too, so do what you like."

Askon glanced quickly, left to right, and saw the prisoner, still crouching at the back of the cell. Embarrassed, he turned back to the soldier. "I'm sorry," he said. "You startled me."

"Well, you sure startle easily," said the man. "The general requested a meeting with you. I was only trying to deliver the message."

"Thank you," Askon replied.

As they walked away from the cage and toward the general's quarters, Askon tried to push the voice out of his mind, but the eyes were still there, staring. He rubbed the wrist where he had felt the creature's hand. The skin was undamaged, but cold to the touch. And just before they rounded the corner that would put the prisoners out of sight, Askon thought he heard a dry whisper.

"We will not stop. More will come."

They passed through the camp and into a flat-roofed building. Two heavily armed guards stood stoically on either side. They stared into the yard and hardly blinked as Askon and his escort moved through the door. Inside, everything was dark. Askon's eyes adjusted to the dim light of a single torch burning in the corner of the room. Papers and maps of various sorts were strewn across chest-high tables. Some showed the presumed locations of the enemy, while others approximated geography of the surrounding area. At first glance, the documents seemed to be unrelated, but Askon was able to guess what they were planning. He turned to speak to his escort and thought better of it. He moved on, reserving his observations for another time.

The two then proceeded past the tables and to the wall opposite the single torch. There was no sign of the general. The escort knelt to the ground and snaked his hand over the dirt floor. Then, finding what he was looking for, he brushed the dirt aside, revealing a heavy wooden panel. He knocked three times, pausing to leave a short silence between each sound. The trapdoor swung open, flopping into the dust. When the air cleared, Askon peered down a set of rough-hewn stairs. At the bottom, another guard stood holding a candle. The man motioned for Askon to enter.

Leaving the escort behind, Askon followed the new guard down a narrow hallway. The walls were packed dirt, with wooden supports spaced every few feet to prevent a collapse. Beneath his feet, the floor sloped slightly. They were going deeper underground. Askon could not say how far they traveled, but after a time they came to another set of stairs, and then the tunnel ended. A draft seemed to come from somewhere above, and the room opened into a wide cavern nearly twice as large as the room with the maps and documents. Stalactites hung from the ceiling like daggers waiting to fall on unsuspecting victims, but their accompanying stalagmites had been chipped away and cleared, to make the cavern a more manageable working space. The room was large, but not tall, and several torches burned brightly along the outer edges.

This room, much like the one above, was filled with tables tall enough that a man could stand at their sides and still be able to read in the dim light. Down here, each appeared to have a theme. The clutter and haphazard arrangement of the room on the surface could not have been more opposite the general's true office. Maps for specific geographic formations were to the right, current enemy positions (which differed significantly from those above) to the left, current friendly positions in the center, and another table at the back of the room which resembled the one upstairs. Askon moved to get a closer look, but a figure stepped from the shadows and met him. The torchlight revealed the general's brush of beard and beady black eyes.

"You summoned me, sir," said Askon.

"I did," replied the general. He walked slowly around Askon, inspecting his appearance and posture. "Your commander speaks highly of you." There was a pause and the words echoed. Askon remained silent.

"As you are aware, the Norill are moving. The attack on your camp last night was not their first forward assault on our forces. We can no longer stay in Austgæta waiting to be besieged. Our only course of action is to attack, hit them where we can do the most damage, put them on the defensive. With any luck, we'll force them to give up their positions near the outpost."

"You are here for a very important reason," the general said. "I would never have asked you to come, but Victor insisted that you be informed." He cleared his throat. "What I'm about to tell you, only a few know. But you must be prepared if you are to complete your task and instruct your men. I will not be giving you the entire battle plan, only enough so that you can execute your orders." The general turned and held out a broad hand, indicating the table at the back of the room.

Askon's movements ruffled the papers lying on the surrounding tables. The cave seemed to amplify the sound. As he peered over the table, the theme was readily apparent. The map showed the ruins to the north around the shoulder of the mountain. It also showed Austgæta prominently. To the west of the outpost there was a red circle; the general's index finger rested next to it.

"This," he said gruffly, "is our current location." He pointed at another map that showed a cross-section of the plateau and mountain. "As you can see, we are approximately one-hundred feet below Austgæta. However, we are not actually that deep. On the surface, Austgæta is actually uphill from our position. These caverns run all the way through the plateau and make multiple forks. Some arrive at dead ends, while others continue to the surface."

"That explains the breeze down here," Askon said, looking up from the map.

"It does, in part," replied the general. "Over the last few months, we have built vents in places where the cavern comes closest to the surface. This work only extends to the areas around this room. Otherwise, the tunnels and caves are naturally venti-lated." He moved back to the map in the center of the table.

"As I was saying," he began again. "There are forks of the cavern that connect with the surface. Some of these are common knowledge—to us as well as to the Norill—but others are hid-den." He indicated a dotted line that began at the circle. "Our plan of attack begins here. I intend to take the Norill by surprise at the ruins. We will begin together at this room. Then, some distance into the cavern, our ways will part." He slid his heavy hand along the line to a point at which it split into three distinct paths. The center and right paths ended shortly after the fork, but were capped by arrows, indicating that they continued through the cavern. Askon pointed to one.

"These will be paths led by others?"

"Indeed, and that is all that you need to understand. I will be leading a force down one of the forks and Victor will lead the other." The general looked up from the map. "I would've chosen another commander for the job, but Victor insisted on you and your men."

Askon felt anger swell at the general's frank admission, but he refrained from making remark.

"This," said the general, moving back to the plans, "is the path that your men will follow. You can see here that it leads west and then turns sharply to the north. It ends at a narrow opening, almost directly north of the Norill colony. Yours will be the surprise force. You will attack at sunrise, and not a moment earlier. Our objective is nothing short of total victory."

Askon focused intently on the end of the path, a small clearing amongst a patch of trees. He turned to the general. "You said that we will be the surprise," Askon's voice seemed to fill the cavern. "Does that mean we are the surprise attack or the surprise reinforcement?"

"That, I cannot tell."

Askon was on fire in an instant. "You cannot tell? What do you mean? My men could be walking into a slaughter without even realizing it." He took a step toward the general. "How can we even be sure you'll be there to support us? Or, how will we know if you've all been killed before we strike?" Stepping forward again,

Askon looked up defiantly at the general. "Another act of incompetence, like at the gate," he said.

In an instant, Askon was sprawling into one of the smaller tables. The general's huge hand was raised, and now it was his turn to take a step forward. "Stay down!" he shouted.

Askon tried to scramble to his feet, but as he did, dark shapes loomed over him. Several guards, who had remained unseen and unheard in the shadows emerged, swords drawn.

"Perhaps we should administer a lesson in discipline. What do you think, half-elf?" the general spat the word as though it left some awful taste behind. "Half a man, more like." Askon stood quickly, but the odds were overwhelming. He said nothing.

"We will see if you can execute my orders. Victor has staked his reputation on you, boy. I have little faith that it will remain intact." He nodded to the guards. "Lead him back to the surface. And teach him a lesson first. We begin preparations immediately."

CHAPTER SEVEN

The Cavern and the Darkness

Askon emerged from the general's subterranean chambers into the light with no visible injury. He walked proudly, eyes intent on the exit, and his swagger showed no sign of any humbling experience. Beneath the veneer, the blows he had received on the return trip ached, mostly at the ribs. He rested a hand on the doorway, staring into the yard. Behind him, the guards stood smugly, having relished the chance to administer a beating. Askon turned quickly and gave them a thin smile; alone—or even in pairs—the men would have been no match for him, but their self-approving looks betrayed their ignorance.

When he entered the yard, Marten rushed down and landed lightly at Askon's shoulder. John paced briskly across to intercept him, and a glimmer just on the edge of sight—near the prisoners' cells—stirred thoughts of a cold grip and raspy voice. Askon split the difference with John, but said nothing as he stalked toward the horses.

"What was that all about?" John asked. "I saw you standing, of all places, next to the prisoners. Next thing I know, you disappeared into the general's chambers." He put his hand on Askon's shoulder. "I'm guessin' it wasn't to make amends for leavin' us in the field last night."

Askon shrugged off the hand. "Indeed it was not." He continued on until they reached the stables, where Thomas was still working diligently.

"Thomas!" John shouted. "And you lot over there!" He motioned to two men sitting in the shade next to their supplies. "Gather up around here. The commander has orders."

Askon laughed, "Hesitation was never one of your vices."

"Nor yours, if I recall," John said."

Askon surveyed the group. They were a fairly seasoned bunch, with the exception of Thomas, who was looking as nervous as ever. Askon cleared his throat and winced at the pain in his ribs.

"I've spoken with the general," he began. "He means to put a plan of attack into motion immediately." The others nodded a halfhearted approval. "We will travel the first leg of the journey together, but when we come near to our destination, the company will divide into three groups. Our orders are simple: reach the Norill stronghold, and attack at first light." The men said nothing, and Askon's voice trailed off. Behind them, the din of the outpost went on, uninterrupted. If the men were waiting for a response, none came. Askon pivoted abruptly and marched off to the wall which now cast a long shadow across the yard.

"Go on then!" John shouted. "Tell the others, and be ready to move." He looked from the group back to Askon and set out to find the remaining soldiers under Askon's command.

A feeble light angled steeply over Austgæta, and a stillness in the air foreboded war. Askon had seen it before. When battle loomed, men went quiet; they moved around less, talked less, lived less. Such evenings stood in contrast to the other sort of night that often preceded combat: too much drinking, too much food, not enough sleep. However, the men of Austgæta had no such luxuries. The previous night's ambush had seen to that.

As the edge of the sun fell behind the mountain, the grating of stone on blade scraped a thin percussion in the prelude to battle. A presence seemed to float through the yard, settling slowly with the onset of night, a brooding anticipation that touched each of the men and even penetrated Askon's wall of contempt. It drifted, wraith-like, from person to person, casting a shadow in the night that softened their resolve and fed their fears.

While the others gathered their supplies and gear, Askon received the finalized plans for the attack. They arrived via one of the general's guardsmen, whose bravado had now diminished significantly. His eyes did not meet Askon's as he produced the small bundle of brown parchment. Askon snapped the paper from the guardsman's hand and waved him along. Neither spoke.

In the gathering darkness, Askon paced beneath a lighted torch, reviewing the maps and directives. There was more to the plan than the general had at first presented, but the new instructions offered little solace. Askon's men would still be attacking at dawn regardless of the situation. He read the parchment again and again, staring for long intervals at the map, which he held in the other hand. With each review, the presence became more invasive, drowning resolve and the will to follow the general's orders. Growing slowly in his mind, the shadow was soon impenetrable; Askon recalled his encounter with the Norill prisoner. Cautious, he drifted closer to the cage, where the Norill were already asleep.

One guard snored in a chair beside the cage door. To his right, a large candle burned brightly on a low table. At the other three corners of the area, torches were planted, but stood unlit. Askon approached, his cloak flowing behind, his hood shadowing his face. He moved silently to the guard's side, deftly removed the keys, and extinguished the light.

From across the yard, Askon had spied his target, there would be no surprise attack this time, no crushing grip nor chilling voice. The darkness made little difference, especially to Askon's half-elven eyes. He crossed the cage swiftly, and a faint gleam sparkled as he pulled his sword from the scabbard. There was a flash before the blade landed broadside against the prisoner's head. The creature fell forward, arms and legs splayed, and collapsed to the ground heavily. Now Askon's grip controlled the situation. He dragged the prisoner out into the yard.

"It's you!" he said venomously, shaking the Norill until its eyes snapped open. "You'll not have the same luck again." He forced the creature's head to the ground. "You've brought this gloom to the camp!" But the heaviness that pervaded the outpost did not lift. He tightened his grip. "You know where we're going and what we'll meet there. Another ambush I suspect." He relaxed his grasp only enough for the creature to speak, fully prepared to reapply the pressure.

"We will not stop. More will come," choked the Norill. The words were the same. And though they had once sounded menacing and ominous, they were now empty. This prisoner had no more hope for rescue than Askon might have had were their places reversed. Askon peered down at the miserable creature, half-starved and writhing in his grip. He raised his sword and brought the pommel down on its head. The prisoner fell limp, unconscious, and Askon dragged him back, throwing him face down in the center of the cage. The guard was awake now and fully confused. Askon locked the door. Handing the keys to the guard, he stalked silently across the darkened yard.

When Askon reached the rest of his men, he found them with lifted spirits. Some had taken the opportunity to drift to sleep, now that the apprehension had passed and the night seemed clear again. Others remained awake, whether for fear or otherwise. Their conversation was light, and laughter echoed from time to time. Askon moved quietly through them and chose a place several yards from the nearest of his men. A scattered glow sprinkled moonlight across the dust, and Askon considered examining the maps for a final time. There was little to be gained from an additional reading, and the morning would bring troubles enough for the company. He rolled onto his back, the stars sparkling above him; stars that he often gazed at from the safety of a rooftop in Tolarenz or in the long grass of the fields nearby. He let his eyelids fall.

"Askon?"

"Yes, Liana."

"Who is that, up there in the sky?"

"That's Heraphus, the hero."

"How do you know?"

"You see how the two stars on the right are so close to each other?"

"Yeah,"

"That's where his hand meets Alora's. You always know where one is by finding the other."

Sunrise exploded around the mountain and down across the plain until it smote Askon's eyes. He was already awake. His leather armor clung to his body, and the joints creaked noisily as he raised a hand to shade his face. The rest of the outpost buzzed with life; preparations had resumed long before dawn, and the company was ready to move.

One logistical issue remained: hundreds of men would have to be shuttled through the narrow passage under the general's quarters. It was a slow process and had already been in progress for nearly an hour. Soldiers walked three abreast down the narrow hall, through the general's true command post, and down deeper into the caverns where a large space opened along a broad strip of fine sand. In the flickering torchlight, the deep gray sprang to life, each grain sparkling in turn. A few yards out, the glittering beach came to an end and still black water took its place. The beach seemed flat, but the undisturbed water was like a solid sheet of glass and black as the night sky.

After descending from the yard to the beach, every grim step reminding him of his treatment only hours earlier, Askon walked proudly to the head of the column. Just as the general had described, the forces were divided into three distinct groups. Victor's men had departed before sunrise, and the last of the general's contingent had only recently vanished into the darkness at the other side of the underground lake. As had become his custom, Askon leaned on John to be his voice.

"I think it's time we set out, my friend" Askon suggested. John was ready in an instant.

"Say no more."

John's shouts and directions boomed along the cavern while Askon addressed individuals. Loose mail here, notched sword there, this one overburdened with supplies, that one clearly terrified. Each was addressed, and all the while John corralled the group and set them in motion. Before long, the last of them passed out of sight, circling the water, into the wide tunnels.

Marching in the dark was a new experience for most of the men. Some stumbled on the stones that lay in the path, their arms flailing and groping in the dimness, though few actually fell. At the head of the column, Askon walked with surefooted determination. It was just as the general had described, wide spaces ten yards or so across, then narrower stretches, and a few large caverns. Long shadows danced and swayed along the tunnel walls, a second ghostly force to follow the clatter of the men.

In his mind, Askon could see clearly the marks on the map, the first of which was the dark underground lake that bordered the general's command post. The second mark was further along the cavern, nearly two-thirds the distance to the colony. This was the fork in the path, a huge open space, at the center of which was a great chasm. But as the images faded and his thoughts wandered, the jangle of the marching company returned. They continued in this fashion for some time until the path began to widen, slowly at first, by a yard or so at a time. Then all at once the passage opened, the walls falling away at their sides. Askon raised a gloved hand. The men came to a halt; all else was silent.

A few moments passed with Askon standing alone, staring into the gaping darkness before them. Time seemed irrelevant here at the bottom of the world, an unseen abyss lying just beyond the reach of their torches. The silence continued, dense and suffocating, swallowing all sound. Even the creaking of leather against metal ceased. After what seemed a great span of time, John emerged from the ranks and lifted the weight, his voice pure and clear.

"What's the hold up?" he asked, unaffected by the immensity of the cavern and the yawning gap that they would soon have to cross.

Askon said nothing, but breathed deeply. He could feel the heaviness in the air and the press of the darkness; it was unsettling, but he shrugged and turned to the men at the front of the line. Peering into their eyes by the wavering light of the torch, he could see the same apprehension. Askon felt fingers curl and latch on his shoulder. He jerked the arm free, rounding on the same side. Adrenaline surged, but when he faced the opposite direction, he saw only John's face alternating from the orange light of the flame into shadow.

"I think my nerves are getting the better of me John," Askon said, concerned. "This has never felt like the right path for us. I suppose there is little we can do about it now."

"Indeed," John replied resting his hand again on Askon's shoulder. "It's a sign of good leadership. You'll feel better about a fight when we get back to the fresh air."

Askon nodded in response and went about preparing the men to cross the chasm. The only method of traversing the gaping expanse was a bridge that dangled over the gap. It whipped and rippled; a filament of spider's silk on the wind. Hours before, the general's instructions had been clear.

"No more than five men in a group, and the initial five must be within ten feet of the other side before the next group begins to cross. The tolerances for weight are slim and should not be tested."

In this manner, Askon and his men began crossing the bridge. Several of the soldiers protested, fearing that the supporting ropes would give way. They had to be forced across. This delayed the progress of the group overall and grated on Askon's nerves. For some time he feared that the company might take so long to cross that the general's strategy would be affected. With each group that passed safely to the far side there came steadily more men who refused to set foot on the planks. Eventually, irritation gave way to hopelessness, and Askon found himself unsure that the company would ever find its way to the other side. Meanwhile the darkness pressed in closer, strangling their determination. When a collection of a dozen men obstinately refused to even move toward the chasm, something snapped inside Askon.

"Run!" he shouted. "Move!" His arms flailed wildly, and he grabbed the man nearest the bridge. "You must cross now, or we will never reach the other side." He heaved the man onto the planks and proceeded similarly with the next three until the rest, fearful of their commander losing his mind, moved of their own volition onto the bridge.

The first group plodded slowly across the gap, but their steps increased in speed as Askon drew his sword and beat them with the flat of the blade. As they reached the opposite side, John approached from the mass of soldiers who had gathered to watch the spectacle.

"Askon?" John asked haltingly. "Is everything alright?"

"No!" he yelled, with more volume than was necessary. "The Norill are somewhere above us. They're causing this—this, *feeling* that we're all having. These men are brave, and have proved their worth in battle. Yet, now they stand, afraid to cross a rope bridge.

We have to force them; there's no other way. And we must do so quickly, while we are still able."

John broke into a dead run to the edge of the gap and stepped lightly onto the bridge. Askon followed close behind, and the two hurriedly moved the remaining men across. Some of the groups required force, as was necessary with the first. But for most, the fear of immediate pain was enough to drive them to the other side. With each group, the weight of the darkness became heavier and Askon saw John's steps falter.

Before long, John's voice had faded away almost completely. As he pressed the next soldier onto the bridge, Askon feared the worst. With each passing minute, the soldiers struggled more and more against Askon. At last only a few remained.

There were six, all frozen stock-still at the edge of the chasm. Askon watched as one fell limply to the ground, his body toppling over into the void. The others did not move. John struggled beside them, pushing against the unmoving statues with ever decreasing strength.

Mustering his remaining energy, Askon burst across the bridge. His feet felt heavy, his breathing labored, as he made his way over the span. Each footfall drummed into the shadows only to be swallowed by the oppressive darkness. When he reached the halfway point on the bridge, the rhythm of his feet slowed. He looked up to see another of the statuesque forms tumble loosely into the gap. Askon's will prevailed over his feet, and he pressed onward, gaining the opposite side of the bridge.

As Askon transitioned from wood to stone, he raised his head and counted again. Only two remained, faces still fixed on the men at the safer side of the bridge. In the shadows next to them was a slumped form, still alive but breathing heavily. Askon gripped him immediately, and lifted him to his feet.

"John!" Askon shouted, though the sound was dampened by the heaviness of the air. "You have to cross now. I'll make sure these men get to the other side. You've done what you can."

"You'll never move 'em, Askon," John gasped. "They're like boulders."

"Go."

John began to protest, but another of the statue-men went limp and fell to the stone floor. Askon grabbed John's cloak, dragged him to the bridge and pushed him out onto the planks. For a moment, Askon thought that John would stop there, but he reluctantly turned and struggled across.

Facing the last soldier, Askon wrapped an arm around the man's waist and lifted him over his shoulder. The bridge seemed longer and narrower than ever before, each step a battle, as Askon plodded to the other side. Several times the bridge shifted, sending Askon to one knee, once nearly toppling the soldier into the abyss. The final steps were the most difficult. With muscles and will straining, Askon fell to the stone floor of the cavern.

"Come over this way." John's voice echoed, and Askon felt himself being dragged along the ground. The darkness receded, and at the furthest reach of the torchlight, he could see the support posts of the bridge. Just to their right, covered partially in shadow, was the prone form of the last man.

CHAPTER EIGHT
The Norill Colony

Time crept slowly onward, agonizingly so for Askon. They told him that the last soldier was dead when they arrived at the edge of the chasm. They told him that there was nothing more he could have done. To their eyes, it was the truth, and Askon knew that they believed it. But his own conscience refused to release him. *I could have reported to Victor after meeting with the general. They should have been informed about the Norill prisoner immediately. Maybe if they had known...*

"We need to keep moving." John's voice intruded on Askon's thoughts. "We've still got to reach the surface before sunrise."

The flickering torchlight seemed to increase somehow as the company moved sluggishly through the tunnel and away from the hazard of the bridge. The air was clean and Askon pulled deep breaths as he marched, savoring each one. Even the texture of the wall changed as the soldiers continued forward. The sharp edges of black rock gave way to a smooth gray surface, innocuous and somehow comforting in contrast. Askon observed faint green striations in the stone, curling like tendrils of ivy. At the far end of the tunnel, a light grew strong and bright; the sunrise had come, and they were still underground.

The clatter of men on the march began immediately. Askon shouted orders while John ran up and down the column repeating the commands. After a time, the two fell in at the front of the line where Thomas had settled into position. His breathing was accelerated as he looked to Askon.

"What contingencies are we to follow now that our timing has been delayed?"

Askon's face was impenetrable, one cold green eye visible to Thomas in profile. In his mind, Askon, considered their options.

The general was sure of the single plan. So much so that there is no secondary option. If the other forces engaged at sunrise, we will have missed the battle and could be held responsible for the defeat.

"Sir?" Thomas's voice faltered. The time between his original question and the second had left him uneasy.

"Leave him," said John, shortly. "Can't you see he's got enough to sort out? You'll know soon enough what we'll do next."

The last hundred feet of the tunnel expanded and seemed to stretch before Askon's eyes. Each step, instead of moving them closer, seemed to push the exit farther away. When they finally reached the mouth, a patch of cloud moved slowly away from the sun, revealing a much brighter daylight than any had anticipated. Askon blinked.

They were standing at the edge of a wooded area. Several large trees clung to the side of the hill, bowing low over the entrance to the cavern. Dark moss gave way easily under foot and muffled their movements. Patches of brush grew sparsely, and the pressing trees at the edge of the clearing muted the distant calls of numberless birds. Askon returned to the memory of the map in the general's office.

Their original orders indicated a route southeast along the edge of the forest and over the small hills that rose slowly to the plateau and Austgæta. The path wound for a short distance until the trees gave way to grass and sage. Here the company would mount a small hill, a vantage point from which to observe the Norill city.

Askon projected two to three hours travel before they would reach the hill overlooking the city. He called to the others in preparation for their attack. "Ready your weapons. If the others have already begun, we may be facing the Norill as they attempt to retreat. Be prepared." He adjusted his cloak and the leather shoulder guard, his legs rhythmically swishing against the leaves.

The hours melted away, and tension grew amongst the members of the company. As they neared their final destination, Askon signaled two of the soldiers who were to precede the main force as a scouting unit.

"When you reach the top, circle the north side through the trees," he said quietly. "Get there as quickly as you can, and meet us at the base of the hill." He clapped a hand on the shoulder of each man, grasping hard. "Good luck."

While the scouting unit conducted its business, Askon made a final pass through the company to assure that everyone was prepared. Swords were honed, bows strung, armor tightened. What they might encounter on the other side of the hill, none could say. The image of his men falling lifelessly into the blackness surfaced in his mind. Askon felt a creeping feeling concerning the events at the chasm and the heavy, despair inducing darkness. The latter, though it had begun as a surprise from the prisoner at Austgæta, now hovered constantly at the edge of his thought.

If they use it against us in battle, how will we resist?

The sun continued to climb, the morning already growing old. The men became anxious, their movements a noisy clattering of metal and creaking of leather harnesses. Some of the soldiers had chosen to open their stores and eat before the coming battle. Others had no stomach for food. John and Thomas represented each group respectively.

After staring at an open space near the line of trees for several minutes, considering the possibility of the scouts' capture, Askon spotted something moving in the brush. It was at first only the slightest jarring of the branches, running opposite the rhythm of the wind. He remained alert, intently observing the motion of the leaves. Edging backward, careful to keep his eyes fixed on the target, he moved to John.

"John!" he whispered as he lifted a finger to his left eye, gleaming brilliant green in the sun, and then pointed to the agitated branches. John repeated the process with several others. The signal continued until all of the soldiers, crouched and prepared for combat, were gazing fixedly at the shaking trees.

"They're ready." John's voice came softly from behind. They remained completely still, hoping for the scouts to emerge, expecting the worst.

The sun crested the canopy of trees, its rays blasting into the clearing. A single darkened form clambered through the last of the branches. Askon drew his knife, and shaded his eyes with his free hand. The figure, now at a full sprint, stopped dead.

"Sir?" asked the voice of the scout.

Askon squinted against the brightness, moving cautiously backward while his eyes adjusted to the light.

"Sir," came the voice again. "We were able to make visual contact."

Before the first question could move from Askon's mind to his lips, it was answered.

"We decided it would be best if one of us stayed behind to keep an eye on the situation." The man lowered his eyes. "Drawing straws seemed the only fair way to decide, and I was lucky today, it would seem."

John stepped up from behind Askon. "From the look of you, none of us are lucky today. What'd you see up there?"

The scout looked expectantly toward Askon, waiting for a formal command. Askon nodded slightly, and the soldier began his account.

"As we expected, the Norill had a lookout stationed at the top of the hill. The edge of the forest concealed your movements, and you had yet to reach this clearing. Had we been delayed, they might have had time to send a messenger. When we came out of the forest, the guards were facing the city. We had little trouble dispatching both of them. They were completely unaware of our presence." The scout cleared his throat, and hesitated slightly.

"What we saw next surprised us. The city seemed to be unaffected by the attack. Norill were passing from building to building with little heed for events outside. That's when we saw it, directly south of the city gates. The field was darkened with hundreds of motionless shapes. It was too far to see clearly, but we both agreed that the battle had already begun and ended. There's more sir, but I think that you need to see it for yourself." He motioned toward the hill.

Askon waved John onward and followed the scout. They moved as quickly as possible, shortening the original route by a significant distance. Instead of sidling the hill and coming up through the tree-line, they scaled the slope directly, moving up and out of sight of the others below. Askon's legs burned with the effort as the three men leapt from foothold to foothold through the tussocks of grass. Before long, they had reached the tower where the second scout was waiting. They climbed the ladder and stood, panting, looking into the valley below.

The scout was true to his word. Askon looked out on a large city with black buildings and the gray shapes of its populace moving about, seemingly oblivious. To the south, on the grass and sage of the plateau, was the ruin of the battle. Askon's sharp eyes saw what the others could not: the bodies of Victor's and the General's men, identifiable by the blue stag on the standards which lay trampled in the mud of the battlefield. Nearby, several Norill worked to clear away the evidence of combat while a much larger group, perhaps three times the size of Askon's own company, stood watch. The fight had obviously been a rout.

"That feeling, in the cavern. We must have been directly beneath the battle," he said quietly. When no one responded, Askon raised his eyes to see all three of the others staring to the south. In the distance, a pillar of black smoke expanded into the sky. The message was unspoken but received by all. They had lost the battle, and now Austgæta was burning.

CHAPTER NINE

Parting Ways

The four figures stood still and silent for a moment, their shadows creeping out from beneath booted feet. In the sky, the twisting stream of smoke swelled into a thick dark cloud. Askon rested his hands on the railing and hung his head, dark hair dangling in front of his face. He waited for the words to come but knew that when they did, it would be difficult.

John broke the silence. "You can't help 'em from here, Askon. And whatever you're putting on yourself ain't your fault." He moved to the railing and rested his hands there as well.

"They knew exactly what we were going to do," Askon said, still facing the floor.

"It didn't help that we weren't on time," said John.

"Don't you think I know that!" Askon snapped. "Those bodies are there because we couldn't cross a bridge. Those men are gone because ours didn't obey orders."

John advanced a step toward Askon. "Don't throw me in there with you. If they were my men…"

"They're not!" Askon shouted, and his hand was at John's throat as he pushed him toward the railing. The scouts, who had remained motionless and silent until now, moved quickly to separate them.

"A few commands does not make you their leader," Askon panted as the scout held him back. "But if it's leadership you want, you'll get it now. We have no choice but to send reinforcements to Austgæta. There could be men left alive who will still fight. You will lead the majority of *my* men there. Only now the path is direct; the caverns were a mistake to begin with."

John scowled out across the battlefield toward the rising smoke. "And where will you go?"

"I will take these two." Askon gestured to the scouts. "And maybe a third. We will make for Norogæta. If nothing else, we can inform them of what happened here. I fear that the Norill may have sent a force in their direction as well."

A long silence passed as Askon looked down upon the Norill city, John glowering at his back. The two scouts had moved them to opposite sides of the platform and were now quietly resting against the railing. The taller of the two ran a knife along his fingernails absently, and the other sat, legs out straight, head resting against the rough wooden poles. John's wheezing, which had lessened greatly since Askon's outburst, was the only sound. Marten hopped from post to post along the rail between the four men. As Askon turned to look back at the bird, a second sound arose, a soft hissing that seemed to pass them by and continue upward. Askon followed the sound with his eyes only to hear it return and end abruptly with a dull *thunk*.

At the center of the floor lay a blunted Norill arrow, anchored by a small woven bag filled with sand. The feathers in the fletching were black, but a strip of blood red cloth was tied to the center of the shaft. All eyes flicked from the arrow to Askon and back again. They dropped immediately below the railing. No one spoke a word. They had lingered too long.

Askon glanced around the platform. At first he saw nothing, only knotted wood and haphazard construction. But set deep in the corner opposite him and directly next to John's head were two thin strips of cloth of similar length and width to the one attached to the arrow. The one on the left was dyed blue, on the right, pale green. Askon pulled the blue strip from its hook. He wrapped it around the arrow quickly and stuck out a hand to one of the scouts. The man lifted his bow from his back and placed it in Askon's hand.

When Askon knocked the arrow, now tied with both red and blue, Marten alighted at his shoulder. He leaned toward the bird, eyes narrowed with concentration. Leaning closer, he rotated at the waist, pulled back the bowstring, and released. The strips of cloth fluttered along behind the shaft, but Askon's aim was precise, and the arrow plunged into a cluster of trees near the base of the hill.

"How did you know to pick the blue one?" John whispered after a few moments had passed.

"It was on the left," Askon replied as though it explained everything.

"What the hell does that even mean?" John replied.

"It's a signal," Askon whispered back. "One color for an all-clear and another for danger. If I'm right, blue is all-clear and they leave us alone." He raised a finger to his lips, still cautious that someone could be watching, or listening.

A slow minute passed, and then another, and on and on. Just as time seemed to slow nearly to a stop, an arrow sailed over the railing and landed in the center of the platform, the blue cloth trailing from the shaft. John plucked it from the floor.

A moment later, Marten descended, planting his feet directly where the arrow had been. He hopped over to Askon who again leaned toward the falcon until he was almost touching the feathers on its back. He closed his eyes, concentrating.

"They're gone," Askon said gruffly. "And we need to get back."

They returned to a company in disarray. Some of the men lay in the grass half asleep, and others talked noisily. This behavior ceased in a rippling effect as the soldiers realized that Askon had returned. He strode forward gravely and, choosing a point near the center of the gathering, addressed them all at once.

"Luck was not on our side today," he began. "We have arrived too late, and the battle has concluded without us. The Norill have begun a counterattack on Austgæta. We do not know if our men will be able to hold against it. Our only course of action is to go to the aid of Austgæta in hopes that we might turn the battle in our favor. However, we must also alert the commanders to our defeat at the Norill city." Askon paused, scanning the crowd and reconsidering his decision.

"I will lead the force to defend Austgæta!" John said, stepping forward. "Askon and a group of scouts will traverse the distance to Norogæta faster than any of us. His eyes see a long ways, an' he knows the most about the damned darkness these Norill been usin' against us."

Askon's shoulders sagged. He had expected John to anticipate his indecision, but the memory of his earlier overreaction caused him to feel ashamed and weak. He bowed his head and resumed.

"The two scouts from the tower this morning will come with me," he said. "And also Thomas."

The scouts dispersed, moving quickly toward their supplies, and the rest of the company erupted into a cacophony of confusion. Questions came from all angles: Why would John lead the reinforcements? Shouldn't Askon be taking more men to Norogæta? Some of the men seemed overwhelmed by the turn of events, others to have simply anticipated it. Chatter between the two contingents quickly escalated then subsided until all that remained was resigned compliance.

Amidst the commotion, Thomas was the only person who seemed to be totally unaffected by the new instructions. As Askon watched the other members of the company talking or gathering their supplies, he wondered if his words had reached Thomas at all. The young man stared motionlessly at the ground for more than a minute and then slowly lifted his head. When Askon could see his face fully, there was no longer any doubt about Thomas's emotion toward the new course of action. A wide smile stretched across the young man's face, and remained there while he furiously gathered his things and raced to Askon's side.

"We'll probably be traveling even lighter than before, considering the urgency of our errand. Is there anything I should leave behind?" Thomas asked. The broad smile remained.

"I think we're light enough as it is," Askon began. "However, if there is anything that you think you can spare for this journey, now is the time to part with it."

Thomas dropped the collection in his arms and began sifting through the various items. He set aside the helm and breastplate that had been intended for the battle with the Norill. The process pained Askon. Thomas—and the other men as well—would be left with far more vulnerabilities than he had originally planned, on a mission of haste with no horses, possibly traveling through an enemy offensive. Meanwhile, John and the remainder of the company would be marching directly into the force that had won an overwhelming victory against the combined forces of the General and Victor. How many had been lost? How many scattered? Askon forced the thoughts from his mind. There was hope that the defenses at Austgæta would hold, but if they could not, would John and the others arrive in time?

Askon's thoughts were interrupted as John clapped a hand on his shoulder, a look of pride spread across his dark face. John gestured to the rest of the company, who were already forming ranks.

Suddenly, the pride softened. "Thank you, Askon," he said quietly. "It is an honor to command in your place."

Askon raised an eyebrow. "That's very formal of you, John. I appreciate it, though it's a little unsettling."

"You're probably right on that." John replied. "We've got business to tend to. It only seemed proper for the situation."

"If I wanted propriety, I would've selected someone else," Askon laughed lightly. "But this company is likely to see battle, so they'll have to settle for you." The ranks of soldiers began to move anxiously while their new commander conversed with the old. Some drifted from the lines, leaning against trees or sitting on fallen logs.

"Get back to that line!" John shouted. "We ain't got time to have a seat." He proceeded to the nearest man and physically lifted him from his place on a large flat rock. "Our boys are waitin' back at Austgæta. We don't want 'em to have all the fun. Move it, now!" John's voice drifted away with the marching company. He glanced back to Askon who smiled in turn.

Askon wasted no time analyzing the maps of the area, finding the shortest route to their destination. If his memory was correct, it would take them just over two days to cover the distance between the Norill city and Norogæta. They could not, however, take a direct line from one to the other. The danger of a Norill offensive was too great. Instead, their path would bend to the south before turning back toward their goal.

"Alright. First, and most importantly, we need to be acquainted with each other." Askon looked from the two scouts to Thomas and back again. "Thomas, this is Christopher," he pointed to the man on the left and then to the right, "and this is Patrick." He sighed at his own lack of knowledge concerning each of them. "Aside from that, we'll have to learn as we go."

Askon reached into his shirt and produced a folded copy of a map. It showed the local area and the path that they had taken through the caves. Near the edge of the page, the sketches began to fade.

"We don't have a map that shows Norogæta directly." He pointed to the faded area. "But I can tell you that it is just beyond this point. It lies to the northeast of Tolarenz and northwest from where we are now."

The others closed in around him to see the markings more clearly. Thomas knelt at Askon's side so that Christopher and Patrick could look over his shoulder.

"We could take the direct line, but that is the most likely for the Norill to travel. Instead, our path will curve to the south. We'll stick to the trees, which might hinder our progress. It is also possible that the Norill have decided on the same course, as they often prefer to take cover in the forest. Whatever they have chosen—if indeed they have sent a force to Norogæta at all—our chances are better in the trees, though our speed would be greater in the open." Askon craned his neck to see over his shoulder, waiting for signs that the other three understood. When they nodded, he folded the map and secured it in his pocket.

"I hope you have plenty of energy. We have quite a lot of ground to cover," he said as he took off into the trees. He could feel the others stall for a moment. Then he heard three sets of footsteps jog into place behind him.

The path was rugged, with short scrub-pine trees scattered across the slanting hillside. They had been traveling for most of the day with little rest. After breaking through the tree line, Askon had increased his pace and the others attempted to follow. The sun hung low against the horizon, already half concealed by the distant mountains. Fragments of broken shale clattered beneath their feet. Askon stopped. He looked out across the deep valley below them. The rocks and stunted trees continued, descending from the plateau to a green space, enriched by a stream. At one bank a thick stand of trees began, extending into the distance where it was obscured by the hazy sunset.

"I think we can make the trees by nightfall," Askon said as the others stepped slowly to the edge of the path. "That gives us an excellent place to make camp and a source of water which we'll need if we're going to reach Norogæta in time." He took a step down the path.

"Wait," said Thomas, still panting. "If we move into the valley, we have no means of seeing what is around us. Shouldn't we have someone to keep watch from higher ground?"

Askon paused mid-stride. Christopher and Patrick exchanged a nervous glance. The four had spoken little since they had departed earlier in the day.

"And who would stay behind?" Askon questioned, now moving toward Thomas. "Would you?"

"If it was your order, sir." Thomas straightened, preparing for Askon's response.

Askon raised an eyebrow, and a small smile moved across his face. "It would not be," he said flatly.

Thomas looked wounded. His head drooped, and his shoulders sagged.

Now Askon's voice was stern and quick. "And why would it not be my order?" He paused, awaiting a reply.

"I don't—" Thomas began.

"Don't give me, 'I don't know,'" Askon said forcefully. "Use some sense. If you were me, why would you not give the order?"

This time it was Thomas who paused. He looked out across the valley at the quickly setting sun, and then back up the path from where they had come. After a moment, his expression changed and realization took the place of concentration. Askon waited patiently.

"I would not set myself as watchman, because my team has a member who is better equipped for the task," Thomas said smiling.

"Good," Askon replied. "And who would that be?"

Thomas looked up from a stone he had been turning over with his foot. "You, sir," he said tentatively.

"Excellent. So then, on this particular command, Thomas, you are in charge. I will return to this place, or somewhere nearby, to keep watch for the night."

Thomas beamed, pleased by his accurate assessment of the situation. He moved forward, expecting Askon and the others to continue down the path. Askon turned on his heel and the others followed, but after a few steps, he stopped again.

"I think you've left something out," he said. The comment registered immediately on the faces of Christopher and Patrick, but not with Thomas. Patrick started to respond, but Askon held a hand out to signal that he wanted Thomas to answer. He turned and started down the path, allowing Thomas time to think without losing any more time before nightfall.

They continued the descent as before with little discussion. Christopher and Patrick had conversed throughout the day, but always quietly, almost furtively. They were whispering now, and Askon was able to hear enough to know that they were considering whether or not Thomas would ever find the solution. Askon walked in the lead, a few feet ahead of Christopher and Patrick. Thomas was several yards behind, visibly considering what it was he had left out of his plan.

Dusk settled into the valley as the four men stepped from the clattering shale to the soft grass. The temperature, which had been searing on the hillside, had slowly fallen, and it was now cool and comfortable by comparison. Small insects floated in the remaining light, hovering closely to the clumps of grass and low plants. Thomas had regained the distance between himself and the others. He moved quickly, stepping in front of Askon.

"We need another," he said walking backwards. His feet landed awkwardly as he tried to avoid the uneven grass and bushes. "There has to be someone to take a second shift."

Askon laughed. "Correct," he said. "I had hoped that you would come to that conclusion a little faster though."

"I did," Thomas said, tripping over a mass of tangled vine. "I just wanted to consider everything first. If someone does appear, how should we signal? What happens if the enemy is between the watch and the others? What if a second watchman is too simple, and I'm missing something else…"

"That's more than enough, Thomas," said Askon smiling. "It sounds like you've put thought into plenty of possibilities."

"Thank you sir," Thomas said, tripping slightly again.

Askon reached out to Thomas's shoulder. "You look ridiculous walking like that. Turn around," he ordered. "I think you should be the second watchman. You've earned it, and I don't think the other two would be terribly interested in being separated." He indicated Christopher and Patrick, who were still whispering, though now a bit more audibly.

"Absolutely sir, I would be honored to be the second watch." Thomas said, beaming with pride once again.

Askon approached the stream, filled his waterskin, and drank. He splashed a handful on his face, washing away the buildup of dust and grime. Looking across the narrow stream bed, he saw the wide grassland to his left that led south to the river Estelle. Behind him stood a thickly wooded area barring the way to Norogæta. It would provide ample cover as they made their way, but the brush was thicker than Askon had remembered. He hoped silently to himself that it would not delay them further.

Thomas and the others also refreshed themselves at the stream, Christopher and Patrick continuing their hushed discussion. The two approached Askon, one on either side.

"I see the point in forcing the boy to understand the strategy," Patrick began bluntly. Askon, lost in his consideration of the forest, turned distractedly to face them. Patrick continued, "However, it seems unnecessary to separate from each other in the night, just to keep two of us near the water."

Askon brushed a few droplets from his shoulder, absently. Now, Christopher spoke. "We have decided to follow the two of you back to the higher ground for the night. Crossing the valley floor proved easy enough today."

"Alright," Askon replied. Then, his eyes and face grew stern. "As for Thomas, you will no longer call him 'boy' until you are under the command of another officer. He is as much a part of this group as any of us. You would do well to remember that."

When all of the waterskins were refilled and all the members of the group refreshed and rested, they climbed the hill that led back toward the plateau. Stopping when they could take in a wide view of the surrounding area, they made camp for the night. Beyond the grassland, the hills surrounding Tolarenz were a smooth faint line. Askon gazed fixedly in that direction, and the sun's last light sunk heavily until only a silhouette of home remained in the starlight.

With the camp made and the others asleep—Askon began his watch. He busied his mind with plans for a counterattack against the Norill. He returned over and over to the feeling that had settled upon the men while crossing the bridge in the caves, and to the crushing darkness around the Norill prisoner. Askon's great fear was that there would be no counterattack at all. If the enemy had grown so powerful as to wipe out an entire force while simultaneously striking Austgæta, then the king's remaining troops wouldn't stand much of a chance.

Askon considered the ongoing war with the Norill, their tactics in past battles. For several years, the king's men had always triumphed when meeting the enemy face-to-face. Even at Vestgæta, when the king's son, Edward, had been captured, they managed a victory. Never before had Askon seen this weapon: the pressing, suffocating dark that seemed to fill the mind and weaken the limbs. If the Norill were drawing this power from somewhere, the king would have to strike it directly.

Night progressed and hours passed. Askon stood and walked quietly over the span of grass and rock to where Thomas lay. He reached down and gently shook the young man's shoulder. After another shake, Thomas began to awaken, stretching slowly.

"It's your watch now, Thomas," Askon said quietly, in an effort not to wake the others. "I'll be awake for a while to be sure that you don't fall asleep again."

"But won't you need your rest, sir?" Thomas asked sleepily.

Askon smiled. "I'll get it, but not before I'm sure you won't continue with yours."

Thomas laughed and rubbed his eyes.

"It helps if you stand. At least, at first," said Askon.

Rising from his place next to the supplies, Thomas made his way to the small outcropping where Askon had taken the first watch. In the valley below, silver moonlight glinted off the stream. When an hour passed with no sign of Thomas nodding off, Askon lay down next to the packs and allowed himself to drift to sleep.

"Askon?"

"Yes, Líana."

"I can't sleep. I feel like someone's watching me."

"It's just your imagination, why don't you go wake Mother, or Father?"

"They'll just tell me to go back to sleep."

"Do you want me to come and check for you?"

"No, I thought you could tell me a story."

"...Alright. Lie down and I'll try."

"Ready..."

"Long ago, before the grandfathers of grandfathers. Before the elves went away. Before the elves had even arrived, there was a great ocean. It was wide and blue and deeper than you can imagine. Under this ocean was a whole

world, but no one could see it beneath all of that water. They knew it was there though, because they could hear its people singing whenever they stood at the water's edge.

"For a long time, they tried to find out where the singing came from, but no matter how close they got, the song drifted away. One day, there was a great storm, and clouds in the distance. The people wondered what had happened. But as the clouds faded many days later, they saw that the edge of the water had crept farther and farther down the shore. It did this for a long time, until the ocean was gone and only the river Estelle was left. And sometimes, if you listen closely, you can hear singing when you walk along the river."

"Hmm."

"Goodnight Liana."

CHAPTER TEN
The Failed Watch

.

A dull crunch, a scrabbling, a muffled cry. Askon awoke, trying to cast off the bleary cloud of sleep. When his vision returned, he looked about; the scuffling continued. Patrick lay still on the grass, face down. Darkness surrounded them, though the faint light of morning kindled dimly in the east. The supplies were scattered, and a haze of dust filtered through the air.

Wheeling around, Askon searched for the source of the clatter. And then it was clear—the clashing of metal against metal—several yards below him. He leapt across the campsite and drew his sword from the overturned supplies, leaving the scabbard lying in the grass. He moved quickly, carefully toward the sound, hoping to surprise the enemy. Bending low, he crested the edge of the hill and in the semidarkness saw three Norill converging on Christopher and Thomas.

The two men stood back to back, swords at the ready. Christopher limped, favoring his right leg. A wide gash sliced its way across Thomas's face, just below one eye. Both breathed heavily, their eyes darting from one Norill to the next. The creatures circled like wolves, and each held a short, flat-bladed sword.

Askon crept down the hill, waiting until two of the Norill had their backs to him. He rose from hiding and charged, fleetly side-stepping the stones and rough grass. He made no sound.

The Norill across the ring had only the time to raise its eyes in alarm before Askon collided with one of the others. Askon's sword sunk deep, effortlessly piercing the thin armor of animal skin and fur. The first Norill fell to the ground heavily and rolled a short distance down the slope. It did not rise again. The creature that had seen Askon before the strike had already turned, fleeing as quickly as its emaciated legs would carry it. Askon bounded down the hill after the retreating Norill, leaving Christopher and Thomas to deal with the third.

Dodging and leaping through the rocks, Askon pursued the creature. Its light armor and familiarity with the terrain allowed it to move with less concern for its footing. Askon lifted his eyes momentarily, and saw Marten also in pursuit. He quickened his pace, sensing that he was gaining on his target.

Instead of heading for the stream and the trees beyond, the Norill veered north and sped into a thicket of thorny brush. Askon hesitated. Behind the wall of leaves, an ambush might await him. He continued forward anyway, crashing heavily into the wall of tangled branches. Blood pounded in his ears while the rustle of the plants against his clothes hissed and rattled with every step.

Suddenly, he burst through the brambles into a round open space. The Norill was nowhere to be seen. High overhead, Marten was circling. Askon scanned the opening, trying to listen, trying to hear anything over his own labored breathing. A loud *crack* sounded across the clearing, and then the Norill was on him, leaping from the opposite side. It tackled him to the ground and lifted its short blade. Askon parried the blow with a bracer, but the Norill grabbed his wrist with its free hand.

The darkness pressed in, scratching and clawing at Askon's consciousness. He resisted, anticipating retaliation from the Norill, waiting for the deafening voice, inescapable, commanding, as he had heard it back at Austgæta. Then it came.

"Your stronghold burns! We will not stop. More will come," it cried. "Submit."

Askon expected to be forced down further into the blackness, but the words had no effect. They were distant, like an echo of an order given from far away. He pushed back against the suffocating feeling and wrenched his arm away. Almost instantly, the darkness lifted, and he was back in the clearing. He kicked the Norill off and rolled to one side, regaining his feet.

The Norill tried to escape, but Askon was ready. He bolted through the grass and thistle, cutting off the Norill's intended escape route. The creature halted, wildly searching for another exit. It turned but never took another step. Askon's sword descended heavily between the right shoulder and the base of the neck. Howling in pain, the Norill fell to the ground. Another thrust pierced its heart. Askon wiped the blade clean and raised his eyes in the direction from which he had come. The sun was breaking over the hill, bathing the entire valley in light.

Crossing the clearing, Askon moved back through the thick branches, retracing his steps. When he began the ascent, a shiver coursed through his body. He hoped it was only the chill of the morning air.

Back at the campsite, he found Thomas sitting aside, several feet below where they had slept. The young man's eyes were downcast, his breathing heavy. Askon approached him and slowly seated himself on the grass. "I assume Christopher is with Patrick," he said after a moment.

"He is," Thomas replied.

Askon reached out and placed a hand on Thomas's shoulder. "It was a small mistake, Thomas," he said. "Many soldiers have taken a watch only to fall asleep."

Thomas's eyes seemed to look through Askon to some point far beyond. "But I wasn't asleep. My eyes were open, and I was on my feet, just as you suggested." He paused and stood up, looking back and forth across the hillside.

"I had moved to the edge of the overlook. A little light was coming up behind the mountains. Earlier I had heard sounds, but I convinced myself that I was just imagining things. I didn't want to wake you or the others needlessly. I stood there, waiting for the sun to rise. But I began to feel very tired. Not the way one feels when he needs sleep, rather as though I had just run a very long way with a great weight on my back. And then it became dark, as if the sun were retreating and the night advancing." He pressed his palm to his forehead, forcing himself to remember.

"Before I could understand what was happening to me, the Norill had arrived. I heard them before I was able to see again. I heard Christopher getting to his feet. Patrick didn't have the same chance."

Askon stood and stopped Thomas, who had begun pacing. "I have felt this as well, the darkness that fell upon you. It is a device that some of the Norill use. It was likely the reason Victor and the general were defeated, as well as the cause for our situation in the caverns. We were directly beneath the battle as it was happening."

"How do you think they manage this? With such a weapon, we might never defeat them." Thomas's face creased with worry, but Askon's eyes were stern, almost cold.

"The source of this power escapes me, but from what little I've been able to gather, it does have limits." He shifted his weight and raised a hand to his chin. "One of the Norill prisoners in Austgæta used this to nearly subdue me entirely. That was the first time I felt it. Then at the bridge, we all fell under its sway. You saw what it did to those who couldn't resist."

Thomas lowered his eyes. "They fell."

"But some were able to withstand it. At Austgæta the effect was much more focused, almost impossible to challenge."

"Perhaps the effect is reduced by distance. You were close to the prisoner, were you not? On the bridge, we might have been hundreds of feet away, even if the battle was right above us."

Askon leaned back, resting his weight on one foot. "That seems the most likely explanation. But what it doesn't account for are these Norill, the ones who attacked our camp. You said that it felt like weariness. That's a very different description from what I would have given when I was in Austgæta, or from what either of us would give concerning the caverns. It was much weaker here, even though we were mere feet from them."

Thomas stopped pacing. "The Norill had a force outside of Austgæta. They were ready before we left." He spoke excitedly, hurrying to keep up with his thoughts. "Maybe this darkness isn't dependent on our distance from them, but their distance from each other."

Askon was taken by the excitement as well. "Some sort of Norill shaman could be the originator, and the fighters that we met work as a sort of conduit for the power. It's the best explanation we have." He pointed toward one of the nearby bodies. "These Norill were too far from the source. In the clearing down there, I was able to resist easily." He looked up at Thomas. "Well done," he said. "If we can get that information to the officers at Norogæta, it might save many lives."

Thomas smiled, pride swelling within him as he stared down at the fallen Norill bodies. It was not the same face that Askon had seen on horseback when they had crossed the Estelle only a few days before.

While Thomas enjoyed his moment of praise, Askon heard the shuffling of quick feet scraping the earth. He turned toward the sound, sword drawn, ready for another attack. What he saw instead was Christopher clambering hurriedly down the hillside. His eyes were wide, and his face showed the signs of recent tears. He shouted as he ran. "Askon! There is something that you need to see." He gestured for Askon to follow him. Askon did so with Thomas moving quickly to catch them.

They raced up the hillside to where they had camped the night before. When they reached the camp, Askon went immediately to Patrick's body. It had been covered by a blanket of dark blue, and there was a handful of dirt at the center of his chest, but Christopher continued to the overlook. "Over here," he called quietly.

Askon turned away from the body and followed Christopher and Thomas. The former, with outstretched arm, indicated a spot on the western horizon.

Horror struck Askon, sudden and heavy, then disbelief. He rubbed his eyes, trying to dispel the image, to deny it, but it remained despite his efforts. Far in the distance, in the light of the morning sun, Askon saw a thick pillar of smoke. It snaked toward the clouds, lesser than the smoke that rose from Austgæta, but far more terrible.

"You see it better than I can," Christopher said.

There was no response. Only silence. And then, frantic movement. Askon's eyes darted across the camp, then looked to the sky, back to the horizon, and up again. He moved quickly, absently, grabbing items seemingly at random. In a few moments he had finished. The others stood by, watching. With one last glance toward the clouds, Askon found his mark. It was small but approaching quickly. Seconds later, Marten alighted on his shoulder. Askon bent low, listening.

When he arose, he spoke as though he were no longer there with them. "Thomas. Christopher. As you have seen, I can no longer follow you to Norogæta. Smoke rises from Tolarenz. I have no choice but to go to them."

"You will be disobeying orders, sir," said Christopher.

It was true. Codard's army did not abide deserters. When they were found, they were tried and punished. Askon would be, too. But the pull of home was too strong. He closed his eyes. "That may be," he said, "but you and Thomas can still reach Norogæta with the information that we have gathered. Stop to rest only at the greatest need and when you are certain of your safety."

"But how can you be sure that it isn't a simple accident?" Thomas interrupted. "You might leave us only to find an out-of-control kitchen fire."

Askon gave a mirthless laugh. "I would not leave unless I was certain. My eyes see far but Marten's see farther. I must go. Keep your own eyes and ears open. Our information about the battle and the Norill weapon is too valuable to be lost." Askon hesitated a moment, seeing the two men as if for the first time, and was reminded of his parents' faces wreathed in lantern light. These men would find their way, and his family, his home pulled harder on his heart than his duty as an officer.

"Goodbye," was all he could manage.

Thomas stood in stunned silence. He watched Marten leap from the shoulder guard back into the sky.

"What about Patrick?!" Christopher shouted. "He gave his life for this mission, and you would leave it—and him—behind? We followed your orders! Will you not follow your own?" Water welled again into his eyes. His face was red and angry. But Askon did not reply.

CHAPTER ELEVEN

The Midnight Ride

Midday and afternoon had burned away with the searing heat of the sun, and Askon crouched near a reed-strangled stream. He lapped water eagerly, cupping his hands and lowering his head in quick succession. After several gulps, he splashed a handful into his face. Evening was approaching and the chill of night on the plains would soon creep over the long grasses, a moment that couldn't arrive quickly enough. Askon had covered nearly half the distance to Tolarenz through a combination of panic and perseverance. Then fatigue had set in, weakening his limbs, but not his resolve. The water from the stream was much needed. His waterskin had gone dry early in the afternoon. Rocking back on his heels, he sat for a moment in the grass at the edge of the stream.

Marten appeared above him and circled downward before skipping to a stop just a few feet away. The bird's head bobbed as he stepped through the long grass, picking here and there at some creature or movement in the leaves.

Askon allowed a few moments to pass before he rose to his feet again. A hazy shape filtered in and out of his vision. He shook his head and rubbed his eyes, but it was no figment of his exhaustion. He leaned down toward Marten, and after a moment, the bird shot back into the sky. Askon quickly refilled the water-skin and, following the stream to a narrow point, leapt across the gap, landing lightly on the other side.

The heat pounded through his clothes while he moved swiftly through the dense grass. In only a few minutes, the blurred shape came into focus and Askon found that he had been correct, just in time for Marten to land on his shoulder.

It was a small thatched-roof farmhouse, with an outbuilding and a stable. Askon approached, careful to maintain the silence. In the stable, one of the horses snorted loudly and stamped a hoof. Askon flinched, but the noise went unnoticed. Leaning slowly to one side, he peered inside the open window. There he saw a large healthy man in night clothes, sitting at an expensive looking table. The edges of all the furniture in the house were skillfully crafted with decorous carvings of various plants and creatures. The designs reminded him of some of the work he had seen in Tolarenz. In one corner, was a well-stocked pantry with food and supplies that would only have been available by delivery or a journey into one of the larger cities.

Askon paused for a moment and considered entering the house, hoping that he might be able to barter with the man for one of the horses. Success seemed unlikely, as the man clearly had plenty of wealth and possessions, and Askon had only a small number of coins. In addition, Askon needed to move as quickly as possible to reach Tolarenz, and a long explanation to a man who likely wouldn't even give him what he needed seemed like a waste of precious time.

A horse snorted again, disrupting Askon's thoughts. In an instant he was decided. He left the man to his comfortable furniture and padded silently across the space between the house and the stable. The horses shuffled nervously, tossing their heads from side to side. Askon placed a hand on the first animal, attempting to calm its nerves. As the first horse began to settle, Askon untied the second. He led it out into the field opposite the house. Then he hurried back to the stable and, leaving his meager offering of coins on one of the rails, mounted the remaining horse and drove his heels into the animal's side. Hoofbeats pounded into the night.

For hours the rhythmic thuds beat against Askon's consciousness. His mind raced as he pushed the animal to its limit again and again. Each time, Askon relented and allowed the horse a chance to rest. *Líana. Mother. Father.* One by one, stars appeared and, though in the darkness he could not see it, Askon knew that the cloud of smoke above his beloved home was growing greater by the moment. The hoofbeats pounded on.

When the first silver layers of light fell onto the wide grasses of the Vladvir plain, horse and rider reached the point of exhaustion. In the dimness, Askon's sharp eyes recognized the trampled grasses and dust where the army had camped days before, but something was different. He checked the horse—which had ceased to gallop nearly an hour earlier—and dropped to the ground. A cloud of dust arose, and Askon's hand passed through, wafting it away into the crisp morning air.

The camp appeared unchanged from what it had been on the morning of his departure. The grass was flat, the dust packed or pushed into piles where soldiers had slept or stored their belongings. Throughout the area, the leavings of men littered the ground: a makeshift spoon here, apple core there, a torn piece of rawhide. But on the far edge of the compacted space lay a dark strip of cloth. Askon hurried over to it, stooping low. He lifted it from the dust, examining it closely. It was black, just as he expected. Their banners and uniforms were that of the king, and thus black with the blue stag at the center. And yet, something about this cloth was different.

Askon slowly ran the strip between his fingers, feeling the material's texture. Many soft threads were woven into the fabric and it was pliant and smooth to the touch, though different from the king's in several ways. No Norill craft had produced the garment from which the scrap had been torn; their preference or skill often produced a coarse and stiff weave similar to burlap. However, as his fingers rubbed away the fine powder of dust clinging to the cloth, Askon noticed a subtle detail, revealed only by the growing light of morning. At the edge, where the fabric was frayed and shredded, red. Distinctly dyed, the color was not that of blood, which would have dried black quickly in the dusty plain. This red was deliberate, bright crimson against a black field.

Whistling a short call to Marten, Askon pocketed the cloth and moved on. Marten, who had been only a few yards away, hopped into view. Askon gestured to the surrounding area, and Marten ascended, circling the days-old camp several times before retuning earthward. Meanwhile, Askon continued to scour the space for any other debris that might have been left behind. Unfortunately, he found nothing, and the morning sun revealed the urgency of his errand. The thick plume of smoke arose between the peaks surrounding Tolarenz and into the clouds above. Askon straightened, looking back to the tired horse. It was ranging through the stunted clumps of grass at the edge of the compacted ring. He stepped toward it, and Marten reappeared suddenly between them. The bird dropped something into the dust and stood fixedly by as if awaiting an action from Askon.

Askon knelt, quickly plucking the object from the ground and brushing the dust from its surface. At first glance, it appeared to be a simple kitchen knife, black handled and, like the cloth, of quality workmanship. But in turning the handle, a device was plainly revealed. There, on a field of black, imprinted in crimson, was the horned head of a bull. Askon recognized the device immediately, but with no one to tell and the smoke calling to him in the distance, he flipped the knife angrily into the dirt. And, nodding to Marten, he leapt onto the horse, spurring it forward in the final dash to Tolarenz.

On his right, the clear stream raced by, flowing out into the Vladvir plain. Its waters sparkled brilliantly, and though all Askon could hear were the relentless hoofbeats of his stolen horse, he knew that the stream babbled and chattered its crystalline music all the while. His heart rose and, for a moment, the exhaustion lifted as he neared his home. Though, at the same time, dread hung ever-present at the edge of his thought. *Líana. Mother. Father.*

Along the clear stream, the colors transformed from brown and gray to lush green with dots of blue and pink and yellow. Only a few hundred yards remained. One last burst before the end.

Tolarenz appeared much the same as when he had left. The little houses stood quietly, warming with the coming of the sun. Around each, the gardens blossomed. Everything was green and full of health and life. Falcons circled above Halan's aviary, tiny specks against the blue. Marten, already in flight above the slowing horse, climbed to meet them. Tranquility reigned over the scene; even the wind seemed still and unmoving.

For a moment, shame and embarrassment washed over Askon. *What have I done? Thomas and Christopher are somewhere in the wild, maybe to Norogæta by now. The Norill could be here in a matter of days, and I've left the only message that can aid us in order to pursue what? A brush fire? An errant lightning strike?*

But no embarrassment or shame could remove the column of thick black smoke rising from the center of the village. All around, Tolarenz was quiet and still. No one ran to the town square with buckets or dampened blankets. No one rang the alarm bell to rouse late sleepers or overzealous workers. In fact, no sound at all could be heard, other than the soft swish of grass against grass. Steadily, darkly the black column rose.

Assuming that the townspeople would gather near whatever was causing the smoke, Askon continued along the well-tended path toward the center of the town. He passed house after house; none showed any sign of people moving within or without. He continued, noting that even the laughter of children was absent in the quiet morning.

Finally, abruptly, the town square came into view and a new sound broke the silence: crackling flames. Askon leapt from the horse's back, sprinting toward the source of the tower of smoke. Beneath the rising cloud, a huge blackened heap was piled. Small, withering flames still licked the edges of the shapes within, and a loud *crack* erupted somewhere far across the square. Horror gripped Askon, and he swayed at the sight of the pile. He approached the charred mass, fearing the worst, when something familiar caught his eye.

Teetering precariously over a carved wooden chair, hung a half-burnt cherry wood frame. At the edge of the fire, the thin parchment partition that stretched between the carefully constructed wooden border had managed to mostly escape the flames. Several holes, some as large as a man's thumb, dotted the parchment where cinders had landed and burned through. Near one of the larger holes, an intricate character was painted. "Peace," it said.

Askon dove into the rubble, ignoring the remaining flames, and threw the frame and parchment aside. Underneath was another familiar object, a chair that had once sat in the corner opposite the kitchen of his house. He cast it aside to reveal a charred rug that had covered the floor of his home. The smoke began to stifle as he moved closer to the center. Beyond, and all around, were the possessions of the townspeople: the tools of the blacksmith, Roland, and furniture from the miller, Eric's house. No community member was overlooked. Askon choked on the fumes from the burning treasures. A fit of coughing racked his frame, and he stumbled away from the fire, sprawling into the path, wheezing and gagging uncontrollably.

After a few minutes, Askon recovered, slowly rising from the ground before the smoldering heap. No bodies could be seen in the great mass of items that had been gathered in the square. He had seen, and smelled, the mass burnings near Vestgæta where he had rescued the prince, Edward, years earlier. The army had been forced to pile the bodies of its enemies and burn them. The smell was unmistakable, unforgettable, but it was not in Tolarenz on that clear morning, of that, Askon was certain.

The square was marked with all the expected signs. Long wavering lines twisted down the surface of the path where chair legs or other heavy objects had been dragged through the dirt. Hundreds of footprints, all of various sizes, had collected around the ring, Askon's boots among them. Footprints or bootprints headed away from the collection in the center of the town, and the same prints headed back.

They had emptied all of the objects in Tolarenz and burned them. But why? Villages had been known to burn large quantities of their belongings if the townspeople were afflicted with a plague or severe disease, but that did not seem to be the case here; Askon had only left several days prior with no sickness of any kind apparent in any of the villagers. While encamped with the military, Askon had heard stories of distant peoples who burned the belongings of a household when all its members perished at the hands of some tragedy, but these cases occurred in lands far to the south.

Pondering the possible reasons that would cause his friends and family to burn everything they owned, Askon observed another detail inscribed in the dirt at his feet. On the northwest side of the square, a massive group of footprints led away from the fire. Clearly, when the task of collecting the items was complete, all of the workers had gathered and departed in the same direction. There were so many prints that Askon found it impossible to discern any single set. It was obvious, however, that they had all taken the same path: the path leading toward the town hall.

A few yards from the fire, his horse ranged into the grass near one of the homes. Askon led the animal behind the house and tied it to a post. Then he followed the prints, looking ahead to where the stonework began and the rough gravel ended. The trees along the path stood silently, as if listening or waiting while Askon made his discoveries. Shadows dangled over the garden and the path now. In the east, the light of morning was clear and strong, but the tower of smoke darkened it.

Just before stepping onto the stones, Askon paused. For a moment he remained still, puzzled by what he saw. On the pathway and the surrounding grass, in a roughly circular pattern, lay a thin film of white powder. Evenly distributed across the space, the substance looked almost like snow, or even flour. But as Askon bent down to examine it more closely, he realized that it could be neither. For one, it was far too warm for snow, and upon closer inspection, it was far too fine to be flour. In addition, the powder seemed to be bound to the stones and grass, like paint or glaze. It seemed to absorb light rather than reflect it. Askon reached down to touch it, but the progress of his hand toward the powdery substance ceased just before contact. A sound echoed somewhere down the path. Clear and distinct, no whistle or screech from the dying fire behind him, it was a voice.

CHAPTER TWELVE

The Knight of Vladvir

Hopeful, yet at the same time wary, Askon rushed through the garden pathways. Arches of leaves and flowers flickered by as his fleet steps navigated the twisting corridors of green. His first instinct was to approach the door as quickly as possible. The emptiness of the town had weighed heavily on his mind since he had rounded the final bend near the stream. But as he ducked and weaved his way toward the hall, a new dread crept over him. *What if this wasn't their doing? Others could be here. And if they are, some of the townspeople could be their captives.* His desire to burst through the door only increased. Any enemies of Tolarenz were enemies of his, no thought, no question.

Abruptly, he halted, frozen in place. A murmur issued from the direction of the hall, but another voice sailed above it, fixing him in place. From days before, when Askon sat waiting for answers, came the voice of Caled.

"I think that patience will come with age for you."

Without taking another step, Askon struggled against his worries and fears. His natural inclination was to enter the building and rescue, by force, any of his friends that might be held there. Instead, remembering the words of Caled, he reconsidered. *If I charge in through the front door, I'll have no idea what I'm up against. And if I do manage to defeat some of them, the others will use the hostages to force me to stop. Some might even be hurt or sacrificed to prove the point.*

For what seemed a long time, Askon considered his alternatives. He would approach the building from the side, where the windows would allow him the chance to assess the situation inside before making his next move. In the case that he was wrong, and there was no threat, he would save the embarrassment of bursting in, the hero of nothing. And if he was right, there might be a way to save anyone who was trapped inside.

Slowly, Askon lifted the hood of his cloak and pulled it low over his head. A shadow, enhanced by the smoke behind him, submerged his face in darkness. Only the two-colored eyes glinted beneath. Then like a green ghost, invisible amongst the grass and leaves, he crossed the space between the hedges of the garden and the hall's southern facing side. The murmur within grew louder as he drew near. A calm voice pitched up and down rhythmically, almost musically, beyond the wall. Without a sound, Askon arose from below the windowsill: first, the point of the deep green hood, then the shadow, then the eyes. The instant at which he could see over the sill and into the hall, he stopped, a carven image so still he might have been etched into the glass.

The interior of the hall remained much the same as when he had left. From what he could see, none of the furniture or valuable items inside had been moved or carried to the fire. Paintings still hung from the walls, including *The Raising of a City*, which he and Caled had briefly discussed before his departure. Askon breathed a sigh of relief, but remained motionless. Some of the town's treasures and culture had been preserved. It was a small victory.

At the far end of the chamber, the murmurers gathered. A group of men, all in black with the emblem of the crimson bull blazoned on their uniforms, stood unmoving in two columns along the edges of the dais where Caled normally took his seat when conferring with members of the community on official business. Upon the dais now were two men. One leaned haughtily on a polished ebony staff that extended above his head, which was either shaven or naturally bald. At the end of the staff, a blood-red gem pulsed subtly, menacingly, with a faint light. The man's garb, similar to that of his followers, was black. A sash of crimson crossed his chest, partially covering the horned bull depicted there, before wrapping fluidly around his narrow hips. Askon could not see the man's face, only the back of the gleaming bald head.

The other figure on the dais knelt, in stark contrast to the dark man standing on the near side. It was Caled, doubled over as if in some sort of pain, his glorious sky-blue cape shimmering across his back and spilling onto the carpet all around him. In his right hand, he gripped his sword. In his left, he clutched the golden scepter of Tolarenz; the blue gem at the top brilliant in the light from the surrounding candles. It glittered defiantly against the deep red of the bald man's staff. However, Askon's keen eyes noted that the blue, unlike the red, did not glow.

"Rise, Caled, Knight of Vladvir," said the bald man's musical voice. It was warm, almost friendly, and at the same time extremely formal; even through the glass, Askon could hear it plainly. Caled did not move. "Surely a bit of rough handling isn't enough to keep down the Knight?" crooned the bald man. "Get up! I said." This was a command. The warmth of the voice had vanished. It came barking through the hall, rude and bestial in comparison. Caled's shoulders lifted as though a great fisherman had hooked his cape and was now pulling at the mantle. Caled looked up, not at the bald man, but far across the hall, directly to the window where Askon stood crouching outside.

"No." The word rebounded from the walls and through the rafters. And though it seemed to be in direct response to the bald man, Askon immediately saw the true intent. A subtle movement on Caled's face, a simple raising and lowering of the eyebrows as he said the word, communicated as if the two had been standing only inches from each other in some confidential conversation. It too was a command. *Stay where you are.*

"No?" The warm voice shifted from angry to amused. "Well, it seems to me that we are at an impasse, sir Knight. I command and you refuse. How uncivilized. But with your taste in company, I wouldn't expect you to follow the rules of a proper society. Those creatures *were* always so alien."

Caled said nothing. He only continued to look directly at Askon, his gaze burning into the glass. *Stay where you are.*

"They were useful, in their way, I suppose," continued the bald man, now settling his weight and grasping the ebony staff with both hands. He looked thoughtfully up at the images on the walls. "Remove those," he said with a grimace. "Unsightly. Improper. The Knight won't be needing them anymore." Two of the men lining the dais broke from their formation and began pulling the paintings from the wall.

"Without the elves, we would no longer exist," said Caled.

"Speak not their name!" barked the bald man. Again the warm collected speech was drowned as his emotions boiled over. He pounded the staff against the dais. "They are filth!" he screeched. "Foreign bodies to be expelled from the host." He punctuated the statement with another beat of the staff. His men, unflinching before now, moved restlessly as the debate continued.

"Do what you came here to do," stated Caled with finality. The sentence hung in the air for a moment. The figure in black had mastered himself again.

"I would not have my legacy tarnished in such a way, sir Knight," he said, with renewed control. "When the poets sing of my victory, when you have become only a distant legend, and I am remembered as the savior of our race, when every one of those *creatures* has been eradicated, and a wondrous age of *human* prosperity is the product, those poets will sing of how I defeated the greatest protector that the foreign invaders could muster. No. I will not kill you on your knees like a slave. You, sir Knight, will be defeated, the inferior combatant for the inferior race, of which you are not even a member. Rise, blood traitor, and I will do what I came to do."

For the first time since Askon had perched at the window, he moved. He stood up, ready to burst through the glass in order to silence the bald man and to defend Caled. Askon's muscles coiled, ready for the spring, but Caled's iron gaze halted him again. There would not be another chance.

"Very well," said Caled, rising from his position on the dais.

Askon crouched again at the window. He could do nothing but watch as the ritual began. The men lining the dais spread out to the length of the hall, all except the two continuing to execute their orders. One by one the paintings came down, carried then to a stack by the door, destined for the fire. Backing slowly down the hall to the opposite end, mere feet from Askon, the bald man lay the ebony staff against a low table. The gem at its point went dead as he released it. From the scabbard at his side, he drew a long thin-bladed sword.

Caled stepped slowly down from the dais, his long strides proud and graceful. He turned partially, exposing his back to the bald man across the room in order to place the golden scepter carefully on the floor. In a flourish, Caled faced his opponent, cape billowing, sword gleaming. With his left hand, he pinched the clasp at his neck and let the cape fall, cascading down his back like water. Askon noted silently that another of Caled's treasures was missing, the green jewel which usually dangled from a fine chain around his neck. The leader could often be seen worrying the stone round and round when he was lost in deepest thought. Askon wondered where it had gone.

"Caled, Knight of Vladvir," called the bald man in the same musical tones. "Lord Iramov, descendant of the greats, challenges you to defend your life against the wrongs you have committed."

Then, in return and with all the dignity of a king, Caled responded. "For what wrongs is Caled, lord of Tolarenz now accused?"

"The *Knight* of Vladvir," and in his emphasis of the title, the bald man—Lord Iramov—strained against his obvious hatred. The music of his voice became discord in his refusal to acknowledge Tolarenz. He continued, "now stands accused of treason, betrayal of his race, and conspiracy to supplant the established rule with that of a foreign power."

"The lord of Tolarenz denies these charges in full, electing to defend himself with his life." Caled's tone was even, unwavering, though Askon could think of many reasons why Lord Iramov's charges were preposterous and unfounded. Caled continued, "Victory or failure now proves his innocence or guilt. Will his accuser accept?"

"The Knight's accuser accepts." Again Iramov refused Caled's claim of Tolarenz, attempting instead to hold him to a title with which Askon was unfamiliar. No soldiers in the king's or any army were called knight. Historically, the term had been commonly used, but only long ago, far before any of the men now present would have been born.

With the ritual complete, Lord Iramov could speak freely, as could Caled. But the latter remained silent, stoic.

"The lord, the Knight? What does it matter?" said Iramov, sneering. "The *cur* of Tolarenz, I say. Like dogs they mix here, and like dogs they shall come at their master's call." At the last his voice had utterly lost its entrancing notes, and now blared as the anger washed over him. His face contorted in a grimace. "What say you to this, dog breeder? Now you reap what grows from the abomination of man's blood mixed with elves!" The last word fell like vomit from his mouth.

Caled remained silent and grasped the hilt of his sword with both hands, its mirror finish sparkling. At ten paces the two men broke into a run, Iramov's eyes wild, Caled's stern and cold. At five paces Iramov leapt and came crashing down on Caled, who was already prepared. Their blades clashed, and Iramov recoiled from the blow. But he redoubled with a second strike at Caled's neck, and a third just as fierce on the opposite side. Caled stood, unmoved by the onslaught. Not an inch of ground did he give in the first succession of blows. The next was all that Iramov could muster, and the hatred burned in his eyes as he struck low at Caled's thigh.

The counter was quick. As Iramov's stroke reverberated off the impenetrable defense, Caled spun and lifted the tip of his blade, slicing upward and catching Iramov's chest. Red blood trickled behind the slashed face of the crimson bull, and the red sash fluttered to the ground.

This only further enraged him, and he came twice as furious, slashing and beating down upon Caled. But the lord of Tolarenz, cool as ice, received each blow in turn, retreating only slightly as Iramov lunged, his sword point driven toward the fork in Caled's legs. Collecting himself, Iramov advanced and lunged again, this time at full length toward Caled's heart.

Again the counter was quick. Caled caught the point of Iramov's sword, flourishing his own in a sweeping arc. Then, changing the blade's direction, he brought it down on the exposed shin of his opponent, just below the knee. Iramov stumbled, roaring in rage and pain.

Now the real assault began. Almost effortlessly, Caled surged forward, still cold and emotionless. Iramov backed awkwardly away, meeting Caled's attacks with his own blade. However, as he grunted and shouted at each contact, Caled's speed and frequency only increased. After several slashes, Iramov was panting, heavily favoring his injured leg.

Then the carpet slipped under Caled's feet. The moment of lost balance was all that Iramov needed. In a huge burst of rage and power, Iramov raised his sword. Screaming, he brought it mercilessly down upon Caled's exposed shoulder.

Only Caled was no longer there. In losing his footing, the lord of Tolarenz had continued his momentum to the floor, rolling to one side while Iramov prepared to strike. When the bald man's blade came down, hissing with the force of the blow, Caled was already rising behind him. When the clang of metal rang from the contact with the floor, Caled stood waiting. He raised the blade and drove the point downwards.

Snick!

The point never reached its target. Instead, Caled's sword clattered limply to the ground and the lord of Tolarenz fell to his knees. Around the duel, six of Iramov's men had raised crossbows the moment Caled had wounded their leader's leg. Only two had fired, but it was enough. Caled, now on all fours, heaved and struggled against the pain, but did not cry out. His left hand reached toward the window where Askon stood trembling, its palm facing outward. *Stay where you are.*

Askon could not. The man who had gone on his own into Norill territory to save a friend, the man who had confronted the General at Austgæta in defense of his own men only to be beaten mercilessly, that man could not stand at the window and watch his leader and friend killed in a mockery of honor, cheated at the last. However, Askon was not that man today. In the shadow of the smoke, behind the glass of the town hall that he and Caled had built with the other townspeople, Askon was a loyal and obedient soldier. Against every emotion that coursed through every vein, he resisted. Caled remained calm, even now, in the face of death. So too would Askon.

Iramov rose awkwardly, his injured leg obviously causing him great pain. The crossbows still aimed their deadly bolts at Caled, but when the bald man had gained his footing, he raised his left hand, and in a deliberate gesture lowered it, palm facing down. The weapons went with it.

"How unfortunate," he said with some disappointment. "This ending will be much less worthy of song." The warmth had returned to his voice again, though it now sounded halting and forced through the pain of injury.

Caled struggled for breath, unable to stand.

"I suppose it won't matter what I tell the poets to sing if I am the only one to walk away," continued Iramov. "Death is not enough, though, for one such as you. Just as it was not enough for the other traitors and vermin you collected here." Iramov strode across the carpet to the end of hall, lifting from the dais the golden scepter, its blue gem glittering. "They say that your fragment," he touched the tip of the scepter where the jewel was set, "has a power over time. Old age touches not Caled, Knight of Vladvir, though his count of years should have run out long ago." As he spoke, Iramov crossed the hall to the opposite end, where his staff leaned in the corner.

Caled remained, every breath slower and weaker than before.

"You may escape time, sir Knight, but no one escapes death," said Iramov, relishing in Caled's final moments. Askon felt sick, but held firm. "My family too, descendant of the Greats, has a fragment. And its power? Death, sir Knight. But you knew that already."

As he watched, Askon's confusion grew. Fragments? Powers over time, and death? It seemed as though he had stepped into the fantasy of myth. Then he felt it.

Darkness descended upon the hall. Not the darkness of smoke or shade, but a heaviness of heart and mind where all light was eclipsed and all hope seemed to die. The crushing dark came down swiftly, almost instantly, and its power grew steadily. Askon gripped the windowsill, trying to remain upright against the overpowering force.

Caled coughed and choked but remained on his hands and knees.

"Do you feel your punishment now?" said Iramov, his voice growing in power and fury. "Death has come to erase you for your crimes." The darkness rose, threatening to force all light from the hall forever. "Answer me!" Iramov shouted, and the darkness grew again. Askon swayed, barely able to stand, even outside the room.

"No one escapes death." Caled managed the words, but his voice was faint and weak in the deepening shadow, as if it had come from some distant place. A smile crept over Askon's face though his head reeled.

"You dare mock me?" Iramov was screaming now, and his voice thundered. It was the voice of the Norill prisoner, only now more terrifying and unbearable. Suddenly, just before Askon succumbed to its force, the weight lifted. Askon's head lolled, and he fought to focus his eyes. Now, in a blackness so complete that it seemed to radiate outward, the space where Caled knelt was eclipsed. Iramov raised the staff above his head and the darkness focused. Askon tried to pierce the shadow with his keen eyes, to see his leader through the gloom, but it was impossible.

"Begone, *cur* of Tolarenz!" spat Iramov, his eyes wild with fury and power. The darkness vanished, and a white light grew in the distance. It washed over the hall, brighter and brighter until Askon had to shield his eyes. Then, silence.

When Askon's sight returned, he still clung to the windowsill. Inside, Iramov stared imperiously down at the space where Caled had knelt. Only a fine white powder remained, a perfect circle, seemingly bound to the floor.

Thus ended Caled, Knight of Vladvir, Lord of Tolarenz.

The Rainstorm and the Memories

Askon slumped to the ground with his back facing the wall. His head fell into his hands, and under the shadow of the green hood, he cried. The first tears were for Caled. Then he remembered the pile of belongings in the town square, and finally the large powdered circle in the garden. For several minutes Askon sat with his arms around his knees—and cloak around all—sobbing under the weight of grief. Meanwhile the smoke roiled up from the smoldering works of craft and art. Between the waves of sadness, Askon heard the final preparations of objects destined for the fire. All of the items in the town hall were being stripped from the walls and floors to be piled at the entrance, ready for the flames. Not in Askon's wildest dreams did he expect to find such sorrow when he reached Tolarenz. A raiding party set to loot the valuables of the richer houses perhaps, a lightning strike or cooking fire gone out of control maybe. He had even considered a small organized force ready to assault the often persecuted half-elven city. What he actually found tore at his heart.

They're gone. Not even dead, to be buried or honored with a funeral pyre, just gone. Completely eradicated, with hardly a trace left behind. Mother, Father…Líana, and Caled right before my eyes. Every trace that people ever lived here is gone. Only the empty shells of our homes still stand.

Clouds had begun to gather, heavy dark clouds, first at the edges of the valley, then nearer. As he rested against the wall, head in his hands, the dense blanket crept across the sky and moved steadily to drape the entire town in gloom. Inside the hall, Iramov's men proceeded with their work.

"Make sure that every scrap is cleared from this place," said Iramov through clenched teeth at the pain from his leg-wound. "We have what we came for, and none of *them* remain. Let this be a lesson to anyone else who would attempt to assemble them in one place. Caled was a fool."

Satisfied with his own explanation and with no response from any of his men, Iramov exited the building. Before crossing the threshold, he called to one of the workers. "Ready the horses!" he shouted. "This place, even scrubbed clean of their contamination, makes me nauseous." And he spat into the grass outside the door.

Every leaf and branch in the garden hung motionless as the gray expanse of cloud moved beyond the lake and across the valley. The trees along the pathway hovered like sentinels. In the square, flames crackled and horses' hooves clopped nervously against the hardened pathway. Beyond, the lake was quiet. Iramov straggled a course between the hall and the square, where his men sat stoically in the saddle, their grim work complete. He climbed weakly onto the back of a waiting horse and spurred the animal's sides, his men following closely behind. The hooves pounded, and the storm broke.

The cloudburst instantly soaked everything within its wide embrace. Heavy droplets splashed across the surface of the lake. Iramov and his men issued out of the valley, never to return. Mist arose from the water as the cool rain mixed with the warm morning air. A clatter grew, and the storm moved. Tiny puffs of dust exploded from the path only to be thrust back to earth by the weight of the storm. Plants, trees, houses, everything in the valley stood soaking, and the rain did not relent.

When it reached Askon, crouched inside one of the hedges surrounding the town hall, tears still crept quietly down his face. The din of the storm came like the hoofbeats of Iramov's horses, too quickly for him to react and with a force he could not resist. But his cloak, and the hedge protected him from the rainfall. Huddled under the branches, he wondered whether he had made the right choice. Would it have made any difference to attack the men in the hall? Might Caled have survived if only the odds had been more fair? But Askon knew that he too would only have made an end for himself, two pale powdery circles instead of one.

When he was certain that Iramov and all of his men had gone, Askon rose from his hiding place, moving slowly toward the square. His boots sank into the mud. Despite the downpour, the powdered circle remained largely intact. Tiny flecks of the substance had begun to dissolve and run with the water down the gentle slope toward the rain-quenched fire. Eventually, it seemed, the entirety of the circle would share a similar fate. Tears welled again in Askon's eyes, aware now that the last remains of his people were slipping away. But the pouring rain already ran down his face; no new tears would show, though his heart filled with loss and grief. He was alone.

Amidst the swirling shower, Askon stood uneasily at the edge of the circle, staring down, pacing to one side then the other. The storm redoubled its effort; Askon could barely see. He fell to both knees with a splash, dark mud clinging to his trousers. With one hand, he steadied himself. With the other, he reached out, stretching slowly toward the powdered circle, now merely a white blur beyond the curtain of rainfall. He let the hand drop. The storm roared. Then all was instantly, unnaturally, quiet.

Bang! Bang! Bang!

Who would be knocking at this hour? It seems early for anyone to be paying a visit. Perhaps it's Askon. No. He's only been gone a few days. You'll worry yourself to death at this rate.

Bang! Bang! Bang!

Well all right. If you're going to be rude about it. Maybe we aren't taking callers this morning. I have other work which needs doing. Impatient guests can wait at the door.

CHAPTER 13 | THE RAINSTORM AND THE MEMORIES

"Líana!" *Now, where is that girl? Probably off somewhere entertaining those childish fantasies of hers. Swinging sticks and commanding imaginary troops, ha! She ought to be learning to sweep a broom and keep a house. I could even stand for her to bury her head in some of her father's books. Unless the king starts taking women into the army. That'll be the day. I suppose I'll have to answer the door myself.*

A thin fog had crept over Askon's vision. Everything was blurred, unfocused, but somehow very familiar. The rain was gone.

To his right, near the entryway, the sun glowed against the parchments. "Peace" and "Tranquility," indeed. In his hands he held a dingy rag which he had been using to scrub the countertop. He felt his weight shift, his body moving fluidly across the living room and to the door. His hand reached out and turned the latch. Light burst through the opening. Askon recognized the visitors. Two of the men that had lined the town hall interior stood in the doorway to his house, menacing smirks plastered on their faces.

"Can I help you gentlemen?"

"Shut up and listen. Pick up as much of this trash as you can carry and follow us."

"Excuse me?"

"You heard me. Do it, now."

"I think not." *Who are these people? If they think for one second that I'll just bow to some stranger demanding nonsense in my doorway, they'll have to think again.* "Perhaps you'd like to speak with my husband."

"That won't be necessary."

And now the darkness descended. The fog still veiled Askon's eyes, but the feeling had become too recognizable for him to ignore. He felt all hope flee and his will to resist crumble. He struggled to fight. Then nothing, only blackness.

Where has she gone? It seems to me if she's just going to leave, that I should at least know where she means to go. She probably told me already. I do get wrapped up in these things. There are just so many intricacies to study. One branch leads to another, which forks like a decision. However, when we make decisions, we're forced to select only one path. The tree can take both forks. Granted, sometimes one fork will die or be the victim of the shears, but that was its fate. But us, if we choose the wrong path and meet with the shears, there is no second branch.

Opening his eyes, Askon found himself near the back door of the house. The sun beat down, though he felt no warmth. All around were the miniature trees that his father constantly cared for, much to his mother's annoyance. Directly before him was the stunted tree which he and his father had discussed on the day before his departure. It struggled for life, but the few leaves which had sprouted in his absence were sickly and pale. In one hand, he held the shears for clipping the tiny branches, in the other, the second, stronger tree.

With a crash, tree and pot flew across the garden, rolling and snapping fragile branches as they went. Fragments of pottery scattered across the ground. Askon felt his body fall into the broken pieces.

"On your knees, invader!"

"Wha…who?"

"Don't speak. This place is ours now. Your breed will no longer be tolerated here."

Askon felt his hands raise, palms forward, above his head. Through the fog he could see again the faces of Iramov's men.

"Take whatever you want. It is all only material. Please, just let my family be."

"Your wife is already doing her part. Shut your mouth before we shut it for you. Like we did for her."

Anger welled inside of Askon, a rage from somewhere buried deep. It creaked and groaned at its own awakening, compounding on itself like some dark thing lying underground, hidden, waiting to be disturbed. Then he felt himself flying from his position on the ground, fury carrying him with unexpected speed and strength. His body collided with the men, tearing with his free hand and smashing with the shears. One of them went down. Then the darkness came. The rage struggled violently, valiantly, twisting and burning hotter and stronger than before. But despite its power and emotion, it went choking and thrashing down into nothingness.

"There! It's done. Everything we have, all in the fire."

"What will they do with us now?"

"If they leave us alone, we could replace it all. It would take time, but it could be done."

"And if they don't?"

"There are many of us and only a few of them."

"You know what happens if we try to fight."

"They'll kill us all."

"They will do that anyway."

"Perhaps if we simply follow instructions.

"I say we fight back!"

"You'll be made an example. Stay here."

"No, we have to do something."

"I won't."

"I will."

"No, you won't."

A cacophony of voices echoed, each adding to the last. The thin veil still covered Askon's eyes, but beyond the blurring image, he recognized the town square. At the center, a fire roared. He could make out nothing specific aside from the bright flames burning across the entire space. Amidst those flames were all of the possessions that the people of Tolarenz had collected, though he could not see them clearly.

Now he was at one side of the heap, bodies and voices to his right, now the other, the voices at the opposite, then farther away toward the town hall, and back to the front near the flames.

"All of you miserable rats, up to the hall!"

Askon felt the crowd shuffle up the slope toward the garden. His consciousness flickered from one place to the next, and so he surrendered, allowing the motion to carry him up the hill as well. When they had reached the appointed place, the group stopped. Askon tried to concentrate, but the images were changing too quickly, only bits and pieces came through: men with the crimson bull on their uniforms; the group moving closer together; Halan standing at the back, stoic and unflinching; the villagers pressing against each other, nervously shuffling, unwelcome contact coming from all sides of the tightening circle; Askon's mother and father at the front, close to the hall, arms wrapped around one another; a bald man leaning on an ebony staff.

"At last, the race with no real right to this world will be gone. What do you have to say for yourselves? Not the foreigners among you. No, the humans who stooped to mingle with these usurpers. What have you to say?"

"We stand together!"

"I'm sorry, don't hurt me!"

"I'll help you. I never meant to stay here."

"Silence! I have heard enough. Beg, grovel, your fate will be the same. The mixing of races is an abomination, as is this place. Be gone!"

Now came the darkness, swirling like Askon had never felt it before. It grew in malice and menace without sound or heat, but with a consuming and overpowering emptiness. Askon felt the darkness rise and fall, heaving as though it too was being stretched to its limit. On each descent the pure black void seemed to increase. Now all light was blotted out, eclipsed by the hatred seething in the whirling mass of nothing. Again it came down in a final crushing burst, and far away a white light grew until his eyes were blind. It seemed to Askon that a voice drifted quietly through the emptiness.

But they were gone.

✠ ✠ ✠

Askon shivered under the relentless assault of the rain. How long had he been there? He remained rooted like the trees behind him in the garden, hand outstretched on the edge of the powdered circle. He stared through the downpour at the place where his hand met the pathway stones. At first he felt bewildered by the experience, moving from place to place, body to body, all within his thoughts. One thing was clear. Whatever power the staff or the red jewel held, the remains somehow left an imprint behind; not only the easily identifiable white powder, but spiritually as well. The memories of those who were lost to its darkness lingered after their bodies had gone.

Quickly, desperately, he rose from the mud and drowning grass. He bounded over the soggy ground, hoping, believing that his guess would be right. In seconds he was there. Kneeling again, he stretched his hand slowly toward the exact point on the circle where he had seen his mother and father wrapped in each other's arms. He let his hand drop.

The rain poured down, and nothing happened. No shift in perspective moved him; no eerie silence, nor veil of fog; only the drumming of the rain and the gurgle of its flood running in streams down toward the lake. He had seen the last of them, heard the last. Lowering his head and removing the sopping green hood, he closed his eyes and wished their spirits peace and rest. Then he turned slowly to face the oaks that lined the path to the town hall. There was still another powdery white circle in Tolarenz.

When the heavy hinges groaned into the room where Caled and Askon had once sat to discuss the leadership of Tolarenz over a roast chicken, only echoes returned. The identical lonely sound, with nothing to absorb it was a cold reminder of the emptiness. The sound lasted only a moment before it died away, eclipsed by the squish of sodden boots. Outside, the rain droned on.

Askon closed the door behind him. Every wall-hanging, all of the art and sculpture, even the furniture had been removed. He recalled Iramov's parting description, "scrubbed clean." Across the wide hall, a small fire burned in the hearth. The flames were dim, but the coals shone red. Nearby lay a small stack of firewood, apparently too innocuous for Iramov's men to remove. Askon placed two pieces over the embers and waited for them to catch. When thin tongues of flame began to lick the edges of the wood, he cast off his cloak and hung it near the hearth to dry.

With the fire hissing behind him, he proceeded across the room toward the white circle. Fully aware of what the circle held in store, Askon tried to clear his mind of all thought. If he was confused or unfocused, he might miss some detail or valuable piece of information. And he had only the one chance to see it.

He fell to one knee before the powdery substance, thinking of Caled's cold, collected attitude during the duel. Even in the face of death, he had held firm, unwavering in his resolve, in stark contrast with his attacker whose every action seemed driven by pure emotion. Reaching out, Askon let the emptiness of the room become the example for his mind, allowing his arm to hover for a moment above the circle. Then with a deep, calming breath, he let his hand drop.

"Stay here. No matter what you think might be happening once they arrive, do not make a sound. And take this. He can never be allowed to find it, or yours. Give it to Askon."

"And this one? You know what will happen if I use it."

"Better that and alive than the alternative."

The veil of fog had returned. Askon opened his eyes and felt the unsettling sensation as his body moved of its own accord. Quickly, he tried to absorb everything he saw or heard. The first voice was Caled's, which spoke as though it were Askon's own. The second seemed vaguely familiar, but the fog affected sound in the same way it impeded vision. Before his eyes now, a door closed tight, nearly undetectable to the casual eye, disguised somewhere in the town hall. Caled's thoughts intruded.

We should have planned for this sort of attack. Morrowmen and I knew that Iramov was unstable. But then again, so was his father and his father's father. It is why the fragment chose them in the first place. If only we had some way to strike back. It will only be a matter of time before he kills all of the townspeople. When I'm the only one left, he won't need them anymore.

Askon listened intently, his body moving through the passageway at the back of the town hall. Again, these fragments. What were they? They were important, of that there was no doubt. Maybe they held great value; otherwise, Iramov would not have sought them and Caled would not have died in order to conceal them. Eradicating the elvish population of Tolarenz may have been only a secondary objective for the attackers. And what of Morrowmen? Askon remembered hearing the name, but his memory was unclear, a long forgotten image driven further from him by the fog.

If Askon is within sight, he will have noticed the smoke from the fire burning in the square. I only hope that he does not see it too soon, else he will be trapped here with the rest. Perhaps he will find Morrowmen. If so, they will escape. The fragments will be safe. What will they do then? I suppose that will be for Askon to decide.

It is possible that I could slay Iramov, appeal to his sense of protocol, to tradition, unlikely though it is that he will let himself be killed. A duel in the old military style might give him the impression that I am the only one remaining. Even if he wins, he might be fooled, might assume there is no one else.

Askon felt his body pulled purposefully around the final turn in the passage and into the main hall. Caled was now seated on the dais. His hand reached down and lifted the jeweled scepter into his lap.

Iramov will not recognize the real fragment, though some of his predecessors saw it many times. This one, this particular Iramov, has been too closeted, isolated in his own lands. He will take the scepter, believing it to be what it is not.

The door at the front of the hall swung open, and Iramov's men entered, crossbows at the ready. Sunlight streamed in behind them, blinding Askon to their faces in the fog. They spread out across the room in a wedge formation, checking darkened corners and behind pillars which might be used for cover. When the room had been fully inspected, the soldier nearest the door signaled to Iramov.

Iramov scanned the corners of the room with a furtive, paranoid series of movements that made him look like a scavenging animal sneaking through the shadows. When he was satisfied of his own safety, he puffed out his chest, staring across the room, not at Caled, but around him, as though searching. Askon felt his hands, Caled's hands, shift the scepter from one side of his lap to the other. The sunlight pouring in through the door caught the blue gem at the end of the scepter, sending glittering points of light to all corners of the room. Iramov's eyes tracked the stone as it moved. Then the door slammed shut.

Yes. Believe, Iramov. Take what you seek. Only one man stands in your way.

"Seize this traitor."

"Lord Iramov, what brings you to Tolarenz?"

"How impossibly tragic. The leader of this so-called city does not even recognize that its filthy people have been eradicated. A fitting response, but I will humor your request."

Iramov's men had reached the dais where—through Caled's eyes—Askon observed the scene. Askon felt his body rise from the seat. Two guards grabbed his arms; another swung the flat of his sword blade into the back of Caled's knees, and yet another did the same across his back, just below the neck. Askon was now on all fours, looking up into Iramov's smiling face. The men continued to punish Caled's body, and Askon felt every blow as they kicked, elbowed, and punched again and again. But he remained upright, though still on his hands and knees. Iramov began again.

"Stop. That's enough for now."

The men retreated.

"I am here for two reasons. The first is almost complete. Those people, the creatures with which you populated this place, they are gone. Purged from this world as they should have been long ago. Something you were too weak to do yourself. The second is, in my opinion, a mere formality, another task left unfulfilled."

"You want the fragment."

The scene, even through the fog and from a new point of view, became familiar. The arrangement of Iramov's men, the bald man leaning on the ebony staff, Caled on his hands and knees, scepter in one hand, sword in the other, all was in place. Askon had seen this before.

"Rise, Knight of Vladvir."

Askon felt his head and eyes lift, but instead of Iramov's imperious gaze, he saw, across the room and through the window, a blurred figure, hooded in deep green. He was looking at himself.

"No." *Askon. Hear me, understand me. Stay where you are. There will be no winning this battle. There are too many, and you do not yet know of what his fragment is capable. Or perhaps you do? Maybe you have seen the remains in the square and all that was left behind.*

Concentration became more difficult as Askon stared, paradoxically, at himself through the eyes of another. He watched intently as the hooded figure crouched, motionless at the window. The figure tensed, ready for a spring, and Askon called out to it. "Save him!" But the words drifted weakly across the empty air of an empty room. The figures he saw were not his to command; he was merely an observer peering through the fog at a moment which had already been decided.

And then Iramov was raining blows upon Caled. The formalities had flitted by in the few moments Askon had taken to contemplate the hooded figure outside the window. He felt Caled's mind, completely calm, parrying and evading Iramov's sword strokes. He felt his hands move with Caled's sword, felt his body giving ground intentionally. Askon considered what he himself might have done, where he would parry, where he would feint. He and Caled had sparred many times. Caled was stronger, but Askon more agile, though they had been so evenly matched that nearly all of their sessions ended in a draw. But something was different now; this Caled, the cold, stoic defender of his people was faster, stronger, and above all more collected and clever. Askon could feel it. Even from the outset, with all his rage and fury, Iramov stood no chance in a fair fight.

Again, Askon felt time slipping through his grasp. Caled made his inevitable counter, and Iramov went on the defensive. Caled executed the calculated misstep, and Iramov took the bait. Askon tried to close his eyes as the horrible sound of the crossbows filtered through the fog, but he had as little power to shut out the vision as he did to command the figures within it. He felt the bolts pierce his chest, one on each side, felt the sword slip from his hand, felt the floor rise to meet him as he fell. Slowly, the hand lifted from the floor, palm outward.

Stay where you are, Askon. This city, our people, need someone to lead them. If any survive, you will be their leader. If none survive, you must stop this man before he succeeds in reaching his goal. Morrowmen will find you, will give you the fragment. When you left, you would not listen, would not see the truth. But you know now; you have seen what one fragment can do. Iramov's brings death, my death soon. Wait for Morrowmen. Alora's Tear is real.

Darkness now. Slowly at first, rising and falling. Then an overwhelming sense of nothingness. An abyss of pure black. However, Askon did not feel fear, as he had when witnessing the same moment from outside the window. A growing peace strove with the pressing dark, an acceptance, even an embrace of an end long postponed, a life prolonged. One by one, Askon felt the cares and stresses, memories and responsibilities leap into the void. And with each, he knew that Caled too had become lighter, more tranquil. Then the darkness began to recede, though its power thrashed and roared. But the roar, violent and strong as it may have been, seemed somehow insignificant. In its place a light was growing and a soothing quiet so deep that Askon himself flung his body weightlessly into its waiting welcome. But it was not Askon's body. Caled had passed forever into the light that rose from the darkness, and it was Caled's own sense of peace into which he had gone. Askon knelt, alone again in the empty hall, in an empty city. To him, peace felt as far away as the clouds which still poured rain onto the valley of Tolarenz.

CHAPTER FOURTEEN

Not Alone

Yellow flames sprouted weakly from the small fire. Only the two small logs which Askon had placed before approaching Caled's circle fueled the flames, and they would soon be consumed. The flames fought, they struggled, sparks and sharp pops communicating their effort, but they receded into the charred mass below and curled at last into the ashes. The embers glowed hot.

Askon too had curled into himself on the town hall floor. Never had the great structure felt so vacant. For what seemed like hours, he lay with only the stone below, the thick wooden rafters above, and the bare walls all around. So much had been lost in Iramov's attack. So little left behind. Askon's mind crept painfully back to Caled's final moments, those which he had seen through both the window and the fog. The instructions were clear; Askon would lead the people, just as he and Caled had planned. But there were now no people left to lead. The skeleton of a city remained, but its soul had passed away. Askon tried to comfort himself by recalling the light into which Caled had leapt at the end. He hoped that all the people of Tolarenz—and his family most of all—had passed into such a light.

Outside, the clouds and rain still swirled. Askon turned from the powdered circle and crossed the chamber to where the glowing coals rested in the ashes. He reached down and placed another log on the fire, watching as the flames sprang to life, greedily consuming the newly replenished fuel. Warmth radiated from the fireplace and Askon relaxed. It began in his feet, then moved slowly up from the steaming damp boots to the trousers and shirt, finally rising to his chin and face. For a moment he sat facing the flames, embracing all that was warm and dry. A full day and night's ride, battles fought, long underground marches, resistance against the darkness, the parting of a friend, the loss at Tolarenz, all caught up to Askon as the heat pulsed over him. He slumped where he sat, and fell deeply, soundly to sleep.

"Askon?"

"Yes, Líana."

"Do you think I'll ever get married?"

"I don't know. What do you think of Marin's son, Jaren? Would he make a good husband? Or maybe Tad's boy, Walt? Would you like to give either of them a kiss?"

"No!"

"Are you sure? Maybe you'd rather make them a nice breakfast and clean the house?"

"No! If I get married, I'll be out with the king's men, or working in the fields. They can stay home and do housework."

"That's what I thought. Maybe you shouldn't worry about marriage just yet."

"Maybe not."

Askon shifted suddenly, inhaling with a gasp. His heart pounded. "Too easily sleep takes the last remaining man of a people," a harsh voice scolded. "You thought the destroyers of this place would merely ride off? That you would be safe?" The voice came again but from somewhere else entirely.

The fire's ashes smoldered in the hearth and night had fallen on the valley. It was utterly dark. Askon's hand moved instinctively to his sword hilt. It was not there.

"Askon, son of Teral. Oh yes, I know who you are: commander of Codard's army, would-be leader of Tolarenz." The voice moved again, shifting constantly in the echoing hall. Askon crouched, listening, hoping to pinpoint its location. If Iramov had returned and Askon was alone and weaponless, he would need to seize even the smallest opportunity.

"Who are you? Why torment me so? Why not just kill me in my sleep?" Askon called. He fired the questions into the darkness, turning slightly with each, sounding the four corners of the hall, listening intently for the response.

"Purely for my amusement," the voice replied warmly. Askon strained to locate the source, but could not. He felt anger begin to rise within him.

"Is it not enough to destroy them, to annihilate an entire race? Now you amuse yourself with me. Show yourself!" Askon shouted. An echo mocked him in response, empty, hollow in the darkness. Upon awakening he had felt completely blind; now however, Askon's sharp eyes had slowly adjusted. In a low voice, he sent a challenge into the vacant hall. "I think you'll find me a worthy opponent."

"Worthy?" rasped the voice. "How much worth is there in throwing your life away to an unknown foe? A pitiful conclusion."

Askon's head swiveled right to left as heavy wooden pillars appeared, dim outlines against the black. "What would you have me do, surrender? My assessment is known to me alone. Perhaps you are the one who has already been measured."

"Ha!" the voice laughed. "I doubt that," it crowed. "You're nothing more than a younger, more ignorant Caled!"

Had Askon waited only a few moments, he would have seen the blurred figure of a man pass behind a corner at the far end of the hall, but he did not wait. In a rage at the use of Caled's name, Askon leapt toward the voice swinging his fists wildly. "Fight me!" he screamed. He leapt again into the darkness. "Show yourself, I said!" He panted and flailed his arms, striking out at nothing.

"The cleverness of the *elves*," croaked the voice in disdain.

"I'll kill you!" Askon roared. He rushed toward the voice, his fury at its zenith, and slammed full force into a pillar. Light burst into his eyes, and he fell, dazed, onto his back.

The figure watched quietly.

Slanted bars of light pierced the inner chamber of the hall. On one wall a low table had been shoved unceremoniously against a well-used desk. Papers and scrolls lay strewn across both surfaces. A few errant pages cascaded down to the wooden floor. Above, the shafts of light brightened, crawling across the floor, passing over the table and the sky-blue carpet at the center of the room. Outside, the rain had ceased and the clouds had parted. Somewhere, over miles of hill and grass and rock, Thomas and Christopher were emerging from the trees south of Norogæta, stumbling to the gates with a message for its leaders.

At the same time, in the small hidden chamber, a man robed in deepest purple sat on a well-crafted, upholstered armchair. His face, cast mostly in shadow by the loose hood of his robe, brightened and darkened as he breathed. A pipe protruded from the hood, and a thin wisp of smoke curled upward, meandering through the criss-crossed bars to the skylight above.

On the floor lay two bodies. A sheet of pure white had been carefully spread over one of the forms. The other had been moved with less care, arms askew and legs crossed, one bent awkwardly at the knee. All three figures appeared as still as statues; the only motion came from the light traveling across the floor and the smoke rising from the pipe, until the awkward figure stirred.

"Ugh," groaned Askon, straightening his bent knee. He pushed an elbow into the carpet, lifting his torso slightly. The other hand went to his forehead. It recoiled after reaching the swollen mark left by the pillar, then moved swiftly to his hip.

"It's still not there." The voice came from behind the pipe. "But if you think it will help, take it."

The sword, Askon's sword, given to him by his father, rang dully against the carpet. Askon spun from the floor, swinging the sword in a wide arc. It ceased rigidly with the point only inches from the pipe. The robes, and the man behind them, sat unmoved by the gesture.

"I suppose that's very impressive of you, Askon," the man said, his voice instantly recognizable from the darkened hall in the night. "Impressive, and foolish. Appropriate in your case, given your propensity for foolishness, I would say." He shifted in the seat, casually resting an ankle across the opposite knee. The bright sword quivered in the light. "If you were going to kill me, you would have done so already. And if I were a threat to you, you'd be dead by now. So either crouch there like a child make-believing swordplay, or lower the weapon and use your intellect for once." The man took a long slow pull from the pipe; in its bowl, the embers glowed orange, casting light again on his face. "On second thought," he said, "just kill me without thinking. Then we'll see where that gets you."

For a moment, the sword point remained, poised to kill. Askon's eyes narrowed, studying the man opposite him. In the intermittent pipe-light, a wrinkled face gazed back. Its deep set eyes were clear, though the lines etched by the years were many. Again the light rose and fell. Blue and purple dots blotched the narrow bands between the creases. A few thin gray wisps of hair dangled at the sides of the face. This man was not merely old, he was ancient. And time had not been kind. "Who are you?" Askon managed, faltering. The blade fell limply to the carpet.

"Oh, pick up the sword and kill me if that is the type of question I can expect from you!" said the man. "Are you so dense? Did you not see the memories from the circles?"

Askon stood, risen from his fighting position, pure bewilderment on his face. Never had Askon encountered a person like the man sitting across from him. The elders whom Askon had known, almost always showed great restraint in their use of language. His father had once told him that the elves long held it a tradition. This man was flippant, incisive. Every word showed a modicum of impatience. Whoever this man might be, he was certainly not one of Iramov's men. If that were the case, then Askon would have been dead—or tortured—already. But the old man was not a citizen of Tolarenz either. Of that, Askon was certain. In a small community, there were no secret comings and goings, even on the outskirts. Then, a voice filtered into Askon's wandering thoughts.

"When confronted by a seemingly complex problem, Son, consider that the simplest solution is usually the correct one."

"I must be Morrowmen," interrupted the man. Askon emerged from the memory, casting it off with a shake of his head. "Yes, that's what you were coming to. Patience is important, but sluggish thinking puts a man into an early grave. I saw it on your face. Remembering something the old man told you, I imagine. That Teral always was quick with an aphorism." The man moved the pipe away from his lips and tapped it against the arm of the chair, settling its contents and stirring a puff of smoke. "It's a shame to see him go. It's a shame to see them all go."

"Morrowmen," said Askon dumbly. "I'm sorry, have we met?"

A long sigh emanated from inside the hood. "What does that matter?" he barked. "I mean technically yes, we have met. But you were a frivolous boy on the verge of adolescence at the time. And I? I was essentially the same as you see me now, an old man of little consequence. Caled introduced us."

Askon conjured the memories from his childhood which now stood above all the others: the building of Tolarenz. He could recall several images from that time, most of which involved hard labor or various bits of advice from Caled or his father. Those memories he would forever cherish, but no introduction came to mind.

"Morrowmen," Askon said again, sheathing his sword warily. "I don't recall meeting you, even as a boy. I have little choice but to believe you. And assuming that I do, that you are Morrowmen, then how is it that you could survive while everyone else…" He faltered.

"Wrong question again, Askon," replied Morrowmen. He pulled from the pipe absently, as though considering what information he was willing to reveal. "It matters little *how* I survived. Though, the actual answer is indeed more complicated than one might initially suspect. This room is enough reason for me to have survived. That halfwit Iramov moves so quickly from one thing to the next that there is always a mess left behind, even in a situation as important to him as this one."

"How is it more complicated?"

The old man's eyes lit up. "Now there is a question of merit. However, we will address the answer in time. The best questions balance the obvious with the complex, and you are still overlooking one."

Askon's patience was wearing thin. Elder or not, Morrowmen's circular questions were frustrating at the least and bordered on outright disrespect for the fallen. If he meant to help Askon understand the attack on Tolarenz, his methods were peculiar.

Morrowmen's gaze drifted from Askon's face to a point somewhere beyond. There, on the ground, cast conspicuously in the creeping bands of light, lay the body covered in white. In his sudden awakening, Askon had not seen it, or sensed its presence at all. Morrowmen's stream of taunts and oblique answers had, until now, fully captured his attention. He turned toward the shape on the floor. The curvature of the form beneath the sheet strongly suggested the body of a woman.

Askon cast his mind back to the memories in the powdered circle. In the vision, he had seen what appeared to be the entire population of the town gathered in the square. He tried to think. Roland's wife? The miller's daughter? She was too young. Some of the families living on the opposite side of the lake had daughters: Shaylee, Irína, Natalé. Askon knew them all, and if the truth were to be told, Tolarenz had few people of his age. Many of the citizens had children, of course, but they were all so young.

"Well don't just stare at her!" Morrowmen said abruptly. "She's not a sculpture to be contemplated."

Askon returned to his senses and averted his eyes, embarrassment rising in waves of warmth at his cheeks. He had exhausted the options. There had been so many in the crowd, and they were all gone. Into that circle, everyone except Caled, and Morrowmen, and himself had gone. And the person under the white sheet. Askon asked the only question he felt necessary.

"Who was she?"

"*Was*? What are you talking about, *was*?" Morrowmen rose from the chair, agitated again. "Use your eyes. She's breathing. Who *is* she? That's what you meant to ask. Because if you hadn't, 'Why are you watching over a dead body in a confined space all by yourself?' would have been a much more appropriate question!"

"Alright, then. Who *is* she?" Askon said, his eyes again on the sheet. It rose and fell subtly; she was breathing.

Morrowmen stood, his joints popping softly as he straightened his back. At his full height, he was taller than Askon expected, maybe even taller than Caled had been. The old man moved silently across the floor, his robe rippling along the wooden panels, as though there were no feet underneath to support it. From a frayed belt at his side, hung a short, gnarled prop. He stood next to Askon and relaxed his posture. With shoulders stooped and head bowed, the aged face drew eye-to-eye with Askon.

In the growing light, the gray brows furrowed, the bright eyes darted left and right, the mouth moved almost imperceptibly with soundless words. And there was something that Askon had not noticed before. While in one hand the old man still held the pipe, in the other rested a dark stone that he would thoughtlessly turn with a curl of his fingers. As the stone rotated, it glimmered, not in the light from the sun above, but with a faint, purple luminance of its own. From deep within his chest, Morrowmen released a hacking cough, followed by a dusty wheezing. He swayed a little.

"You must accept that there are some things that I cannot say. Some things for which you are not prepared. At this moment, I can tell you that she is incredibly important, possibly the most important. I can tell you also that she is indeed from Tolarenz, though you would not recognize her."

Askon looked from Morrowmen to the body with a raised eyebrow. Without thinking, he reached toward the sheet. There were no citizens of Tolarenz that he would not recognize.

Crack!

In the span of time between the quizzical look and the stretch toward the body, Morrowmen had pinched the pipe between his teeth, drawn the prop from his belt, and brought it down in a stinging blow across Askon's wrist. A snarl appeared to accompany the arched eyebrow, and Askon would have let his anger take control. But the prop rounded, whistling in the air, the knot at the end colliding solidly with his forehead. He stared back in disbelief. A weak laugh escaped.

"What was that?" he asked.

"That was a reminder. When you act like a child, you should expect to be treated as such." The prop slid back into the belt, and the stone turned in Morrowmen's hand. "As I said, you would not recognize her. I realize that you think you know everyone in Tolarenz, and you might. But that is not the issue at hand. Were you to pull back that sheet, not only would you be deeply scarred by the sight, you would risk undoing everything I have done to save her."

Askon rubbed his wrist where the cane had left a red welt. His head throbbed, the previous night's injury from the pillar reawakened by the knotted end of the cane. "Save her? Do you mean you were able to rescue someone from Iramov?"

Morrowmen shook his head slowly. "No, not from him. From that fate no normal person can escape." He moved around the sheet so that he could face Askon. "When I found her, burns covered most of her body. Only shreds of charred clothing remained, painfully embedded in the skin. I had to remove the foreign material, which is another good reason why you shouldn't be pulling back that sheet anytime soon." He smiled crookedly. Askon's face flushed, and he looked away from the body on the floor. "She may have run straight into the fire with all of the belongings, hoping to retrieve something. More likely, she refused to help Iramov, and he or his men threw her into the flames and left her for dead." Morrowmen crouched and ran his hand slowly over the sheet, a hairsbreadth away from actual contact. "I brought her here and tended to her wounds. She will make a full recovery, if you can keep your curiosity to yourself. The added trauma of being burned alive will affect her psychologically, of course, as it would anyone."

Askon, crouching as well, raised his hand in the same mock-caress which Morrowmen had exhibited.

"A nice gesture," said Morrowmen. "Useless, but nice."

Askon looked up, offended by the old man's harsh words. "You just did the same thing. Why, when you have already done so, is it useless coming from me?"

Morrowmen stood again with an effort. His blotched, ancient hand turned the small purple stone then motioned toward the armchairs on the opposite wall. "That is a larger and more important question than you realize, Askon." He crossed the room and reached into a small cabinet. Again, he motioned for Askon to sit. And Askon did.

CHAPTER FIFTEEN

Fragments

"A little food and drink will help with understanding and thought-ful response," said Morrowmen as he produced two small loaves of bread and a hunk of cheese on a polished wooden plate. He set the food on the floor between the chairs. Then from a shelf nearby, he collected two cups and a sparkling decanter filled to half with golden liquid. He poured a small amount into each cup. Handing one of them to Askon, he turned to take his seat.

"To Caled," Askon said, raising the cup. "The food reminds me of him. He had the same custom of offering a meal when discussing important matters."

"So he did," Morrowmen replied. "Though I daresay, he ac-quired that particular practice from me." He smiled, a faraway smile that gazed back an uncounted number of years. "To Caled."

Askon took one of the loaves into his hands, awkwardly setting the cup on the ground where the plate also rested. He tore the bread into halves and handed one to Morrowmen. "So, why is my gesture useless and yours somehow not?"

"It is not in the gesture that the difference lies. I am old, Askon, as anyone can easily see. What you cannot see, is exactly how long it is since I was brought into this world. The year of my birth was long before anyone you know or have known in your short lifetime. I remember your grandfather when he was a boy. Not so different was he from when I met you for the first time, which you conveniently do not remember."

Although Morrowmen had adopted a formal air, the old sarcasm lingered. Askon ignored it. "You knew my grandfather? Were you also a boy at that time?"

Morrowmen took a sip from the cup. His pipe rested on the ground next to the plate, extinguished. "When your grandfather was a boy, I was much the same as you see me now."

"Old and of little consequence?" Askon offered playfully. He smiled, and Morrowmen returned one of his own.

"Yes," he said. "In that time period I was of little consequence to the events which took place. As you know, your grandfather's life was marked by the Scouring of Vladvir. A time which I thought had passed."

"As did we," replied Askon. "My father told me the stories, though he always said that it began long before."

"It did. The Greats, as they used to call themselves, voted to remove all elvish presence from the kingdom. In the rural areas, this was an easy declaration to make on account of the support from the relatively uneducated population, though the elf-kind— your kind—were difficult to locate. In the cities, the people were at first more reluctant, claiming equality and defending their friends and neighbors. But they came around. After years of propaganda and misinformation, most men would turn in an elf or even a suspected elf on a moment's notice."

"I have heard the stories," said Askon "but what does my grandfather have to do with her?" He pointed to the shape on the floor.

"A fair point, though you still refuse to be patient. I suppose you are owed a direct explanation, however irritated I am at your interruptions." Morrowmen lowered the cup and bread. When he began, his hands moved fluidly, as if their dance would help to articulate his words.

"I use the example of your grandfather merely to indicate one of many time periods through which I have lived. I was born not only many years ago, but many lifetimes, many generations ago, just before the time of the Great Darkness."

Askon choked on a piece of cheese and swallowed hard. "That's impossible!" he laughed. "Next you'll tell me that you saw the coming of the elves."

"I did see their coming, and what they were capable of. They wiped the forces of the enemy clean from Vladvir. We owe them our existence. Their weapons, their armor: it was all more advanced than even our best designers and smiths could imagine. The enemy didn't stand a chance, and the people were awed by them. However, another faction feared their power, the seeds of what would eventually lead to the Scouring. That faction insisted that no other elves be allowed to enter. We had no reason to believe any more of them would appear, and so—as a compromise—we accepted."

"Are you saying that you know how the elves came into our world?" Askon sat up in the chair, listening like a child eager for a bedtime story.

"I do. Many did at one time, but the specifics were given to only a few in those days: myself and four others."

"Who were they? What did they do to bring the elves here? How can you still be alive?!" Askon stammered.

Morrowmen lowered his head. "I'll get to that," he said irritably. "Three of the others—the ones who would eventually give themselves the title of the Greats—were nobility of the kingdom. The highest of them was Lord Codard."

"What?!" Askon's eyes snapped open wide.

"Stop with the interjections, Askon!" Morrowmen fired back. "No, he is not the same Codard. That name, like me, is many generations old. Not all of the five have survived the years as I have. "He lowered his head again, trying to relocate the thread of his story. "The two others were lords as well: Iramov and Apopsé. Iramov's descendant, you have seen here. The man bearing Apopsé's name lives to the south, far down the river Estelle."

"Yes," said Askon. "The king allowed his grandfather to begin a settlement of his own as long as it paid tribute to Codard. The

South Kingdom has done so, and never showed any aggression or any desire to claim land in Vladvir. It's a merchant's kingdom."

"Quite true," responded Morrowmen. His eyes grew grave and reverent. "The last of the five was a knight. He came from a small village, and it was said that he descended from a noble line going back into time as far before the Great Darkness as my birth is from yours. It was he who brought the elves into Vladvir. His name was Caled, and he found *it*: the object that would generate so much good and so much evil. He found Alora's Tear. He too uncovered the instructions for using it—tucked away in a lowly farmhouse of all places."

Askon was indignant. He shook his head. "So, you're telling me that the man who helped build Tolarenz lived for hundreds of years, still looked like he was in the prime of his life, and not only sympathized with the elves, but also brought them into this world using a magical jewel from a children's fairytale?" He chuckled and leaned back in the chair, sipping noisily on his drink. "Did he find it by the roadside while harvesting pixie dust from the back of his unicorn? Or did he only need a magic wand?" He laughed again, but in his derision he did not hear the whistling.

Crack!

"Fool!" exclaimed Morrowmen. "Leave the commentary to someone with a little more sense."

Askon sat, again dumbfounded by the speed with which the old man applied the stick. He tried to ignore the anger at being struck like a petulant child.

Morrowmen began again. "It seems that you need more than the wise words of an elder to convince you. Considering your previous demonstrations of…" he paused, "intellect. I didn't expect you to be so discerning." Askon watched as the prop slid back into the belt. "Perhaps Caled wasn't completely wrong in his choice of successor. In light of this, a physical proof for your benefit, or at least a reprieve for my walking stick."

Morrowmen reached into the folds of his robe to retrieve the stone which Askon had seen when he awoke. The withered hand looked waxy and dead against the deep, glowing purple. The bony fingers sprang back, holding the stone palm upward; the light inside pulsed as if breathing.

"This is a fragment of Alora's Tear," he said solemnly. "Only four knew of its existence after Caled's death; now you make five once again."

"That stone is the size of a dinner roll, Morrowmen," said Askon. "How can it be a fragment of a tear. Such a thing would be tiny."

"Indeed it is," said Morrowmen. And in a soft, fluid movement, he passed his other hand over the stone. Askon heard a minute mechanical *click* and watched as it popped open like a steamed clamshell. Inside, a gem rested snugly, glowing now bright, now dim, a vivid purple. Morrowmen snapped the case shut and went on with his explanation.

"As you can see," he said. "It is small, but still not the appropriate size for the fraction of a human tear. The original gem which Caled used to call upon the elves was larger than one would expect. Greater than a robin's egg, but lesser than a chicken's, I used to say. Caled hated the common terminology. He was always so intent on formality." Morrowmen smiled and shook his head. "Back then, rightly I believe, I theorized that the real tear that fell from Alora's cheek was encased by crystal growth, layer upon layer. It still had the general teardrop shape, when it was whole. After dividing the jewel, we assumed that the centerpiece housed the tear proper."

Askon tried to envision, based on the fragment in the stone case, what the original must have looked like. The process must have shown on his face because Morrowmen stood abruptly, pocketing the stone. "Hopeless. One minute you think not at all, the next you are a ponderous sluggard. Why don't I illustrate, so that your thoughts can keep up." He walked to the opposite side of the room and retrieved a leaf of paper and an ink bottle and quill from the desk, placing both on a nearby table. He shot Askon a glare and accompanied it with a sigh. Askon leapt from his seat to help the old man move the table between the chairs. Morrowmen went to work sketching and re-sketching the original tear. Askon busied himself with the bread and cheese and cup of brandy. Soon the depiction was finished.

On the page Askon saw what appeared to be a large teardrop, divided into pieces. At the center was a rectangle, inside of which was a second, much smaller teardrop, representing the original tear. Inside the rectangle Morrowmen had written the word "Sight." The three rounded edges of the large teardrop had been separated from the rectangle's sides. On the left was the word

"Life," on the right "Death," and at the bottom "Space." At the top of the image, the pointed tip of the teardrop, the final separation was made. Above was the word "Time." Five fragments for the five Greats with the center housing the "tear proper" as Morrowmen had described. Askon stared for a moment at the shapes on the page.

"So the fragment labeled 'Time' must be the one that you carry in that stone," said Askon excitedly.

Morrowmen rolled his eyes. "A fair guess I suppose, but wrong."

"Why? If you've been alive for hundreds of years, that fragment must have something to do with time."

"Ah, there you hit the mark, or near it at least. I hope your swordsmanship isn't so approximate. The key word is 'alive', Askon. Watch." He lifted the stone from his pocket once again, then reached to the shelf behind him and retrieved a small, polished looking glass. He raised it to Askon's face.

Askon looked into the mirror, his own reflection stared back. He was stung at once by what he saw there, both the face of his mother and that of his father: mother in the dark hair and father in the points of his ears. But nowhere was the melding of the two parents—the two races—as clear as in the eyes, one green and one blue. Above, a deep yellow-gray bruise rose from the smooth skin of his brow. The drink had taken the pain away, but he still felt the injury's faint pulse.

Morrowmen slowly lifted the stone, drawing it level with Askon's forehead. Without touching him, Morrowmen moved the stone over the bruise on his brow. The sunken eyes closed for a moment and the old man waved the stone back and forth over Askon's face. Askon felt a slight warmth and prickling tingle as the aged hand passed before his eyes. Then Morrowmen lowered hand and stone.

In the mirror the eyes, the blue and the green, stared back. They made their way inevitably to the bruised area above. Askon recoiled. The mark was gone. No swelling or discoloration remained; even the light scrapes left by the rough wooden pillar had vanished. Morrowmen set the looking glass face-down on the table.

"The Life fragment, Askon. That mark will not return," he said. "Unless my walking stick requires additional exercise, that is."

Askon touched his forehead where the injury had been only moments before. He tapped with fingers, pressed, rubbed, knuckled the area, but he was fully and completely healed. It was as if the blows had never happened.

"Amazing, I know," said Morrowmen. "But not without cost. Though you are good as new, insofar as your forehead goes, the price that the fragment extracts is in age. Your wound was small, and thus you have aged only a little. Based on the lump that pillar gave you, I would guess you lost a couple hours from your life, maybe only minutes, if you want to count it in such a way. The fragment accelerates the healing process but the subject gets older as a result. If the damage had been more serious, you would have needed time to rest and recover, but you would indeed recover flawlessly."

A wave of recognition pushed itself across Askon's face. "You've used the fragment on yourself, then?" he asked.

"I have, but only for minor cuts and such, maybe a broken bone at some point. It has been so long, I can't recall all the times I've needed it." He rubbed an arm, remembering an old injury. "No, the effect of carrying the fragment is what has kept me alive all these years. The possessor of this piece of the Tear is given the gift of life as long as they carry it. For me, that is a very long span of time."

Askon sat up again, considering the nearly unfathomable age of the man sitting beside him. Many questions arose in his mind: questions about the powdery circles, about the Scouring, the Great Darkness, the elves. He settled finally on Caled. This might be his only chance to understand the life his leader and mentor lived before Tolarenz, or Askon, or any of them.

"How then, did Caled's fragment work? I assume that Iramov has the Death fragment. Wouldn't Caled have been able to fight back using his own in some way? I saw, in the memory and from the window, that he carried the Scepter of Tolarenz. It has a gem at its point, and Iramov carried it off once Caled was…" he hesitated, "gone."

Morrowmen's entire face lit up at this, a twisted distortion of joy on the wrinkled and creased visage. "Ha!" he croaked, and Askon was reminded of the same voice, crow-like in the darkness the night before. "Then there is some intelligence latent in that reckless mind of yours! I was beginning to wonder if the war stories about you exaggerated your tactical prowess when in reality your victories were blind luck driven by emotion. Certainly, you are indeed emotional, but I had hoped that some of your father's analytical nature had trickled down through the soldier's filter that you so often wear."

Askon sighed. "Is it necessary to criticize me at every step in the process?"

"Of course," Morrowmen laughed again. "You see, the adage goes that with age comes wisdom. I find that as the years pass, many things wither and fall away. My ability to berate the ignorant, specifically the young adults who feel some sort of mastery of their world, only increases. And in a wonderful twist of fate, the pleasure I get from exercising this ability increases proportionally to the number of years that I have been alive. So, yes. I do have to criticize you at every step. Remember, though, I tripped and fell on many of the same steps long before you did." He took a sip of the brandy and paused for a moment, thinking.

"As I said, all good questions concerning the Scepter and whatnot. Good observations. Wrong again, but good. I should address first, as you have probably guessed, that Caled carried the Time fragment. It has a more passive nature than the other fragments, though some qualities come and go as the pieces change hands. Iramov's father, for instance, would not have been able to perform the acts that you saw. That fragment, the Death fragment, as you rightly hit it, seems to feed off anger or possibly madness. I have never been sure. Iramov's father had neither of these. He was quite reasonable." Morrowmen took a small bite from the now significantly diminished cheese. "And Caled? He was always reasonable, sometimes irritatingly so. He was calm, collected, and the fragment seemed to reflect that disposition. The quality it presented was similar to the Life fragment that I carry. As long as Caled held it, he never aged. He was a young man, probably near your age, when he found the complete Tear. Ten years later, when the five decided to divide it, he was in his prime, and looked almost exactly as he did when you knew him. Did it not ever occur to you that you had grown your whole life, while he stayed the same?"

Askon lifted his own cup to his lips. "To a child or even an adolescent, adults appear to change very little, if at all. I suppose now it seems odd, looking back. To answer your question though, no, I didn't notice."

"A fair point," replied Morrowmen through a piece of bread, "that bit about children and adults." He gulped it down. "When you are as far away from childhood as I am, it becomes difficult to remember such things." Reaching for the cup, he found it dry. The bright eyes wandered to the decanter, then back to the cup, apparently thinking better of it.

"On the point of fighting back, using the fragment to do so, that is, I think that Caled would have found the thought repulsive. You saw what Iramov looked like when he exercised the power of the Death fragment. Caled would never have wanted to appear as such."

"But you use the Life fragment." Askon pointed to the sheet on the floor.

"I do," said Morrowmen. "I did. Caled might not have done so. It would have troubled him greatly to make such a decision in the short time that I had to make it. You see, Caled was thoughtful, often too thoughtful, which is why I have demanded and will continue to demand balance from you. Think, but not too much, or you'll find yourself in a powdered circle."

The sun had traveled slowly across the sky, and in so doing, the bars of light traversed the floor. He wondered if the passage of the sun mattered at all when a person, someone like Morrowmen, someone like Caled, had seen so many risings and settings.

"I apologize," said Morrowmen quietly. "For you, the grief of his passing is great. For me, the saying about living a long and full life could not be more apt than with Caled. Even I cannot claim the same for myself. He remained young, capable of taking risks yet often chose the safe road, though not with Tolarenz. There he was always resolute. I, on the other hand, have been forced to be more careful and am less capable of doing great deeds."

For the first time, Askon saw the facade fall and an air of sadness pass over the old man's face. Those eyes had seen much, and Askon pitied him for the times that he would have been forced to stand by, unable to help due to his ever aging, and for many years ancient, body.

"What about the Scepter?" Askon prodded, gently.

Morrowmen laughed, a sound so full of mirth that Askon could hardly believe it came from the sad old man he had observed only a moment before. The laughter continued until small tears welled around the edges of the bright eyes. "Oh that was brilliant, and it worked like a charm," he said gasping. "That imbecile Iramov had no idea. The Scepter has nothing whatever to do with the Tear or its fragments. Caled, in all his thoughtful planning, knew that Iramov was coming. Not soon enough to evacuate, mind you, but with a bit of time to spare.

We have been watching him, observing his movements, as we do with all of the fragment holders. What we didn't account for, was the power that this particular Iramov is able to wield. As I said, his predecessor showed no ability to command the fragment, and we incorrectly assumed that he would be the same. We were wrong about that. But Caled was right in his belief that Iramov would come to take the fragment, and he had already planned for you to lead Tolarenz. It was a good plan, a perfect sleight of hand. Caled gave me the Time fragment, Askon."

Askon stood, backing away from the chairs. "Wait," he said nervously. But the story could not be stopped.

"He also knew that you would see the smoke and return here. I don't think he realized that you would be so quick. You almost ended up dead yourself, had you been any earlier." Morrowmen rose from the chair, and took a step toward Askon. "He left the Time fragment in my care. In his mind, he had already given it to you." The pale hand glided swiftly back to the pocket where he kept the Life fragment. In a split second the hand returned. The palm pointed toward the skylight; down into the open air below dangled a silver chain. At its end hung a brilliant green jewel. "And now," said the old man, "you have it."

Askon reached toward the sparkling gem. Just before his outstretched fingers made contact with the shinning surface, a faint pulse emanated from deep inside. The fragment's glow breathed bright, and Askon's hand closed around it.

CHAPTER SIXTEEN
Saying Goodbye

Askon's hand clasped the pulsing gem, green light seeping through his fingers. The room felt suddenly cooler. The air seemed lighter; breaths came easier. The aches and pains of travel softened. And for a moment, Morrowmen's trembling hand became still, moving only slowly as he released the fine silver chain. It fell, swinging from side to side below Askon's closed fist, and he felt for the first time the weight of the Time fragment. It was much heavier than it should have been, considering its size. But with it in his possession, Askon himself felt lighter, everything within his sight, sharper, more focused. He released the fragment and looped the chain over his head, the metal like ice on his skin. The jewel pulsed, very slowly, so slowly that the brighter and darker shades of green seemed only a trick of the light glinting off its many facets.

A low, muffled groan sounded in the small space. Under the white sheet, the body shifted, twisting this way and that. She was awake.

"Alright, no more time," said Morrowmen hurriedly. He pushed Askon away from the body. "She needs my care, and mine alone. There is more to this than waving a hand over the affected area." He continued to push until Askon's back pressed up against the wall at the far side of the room. "Out!" Morrowmen shouted with a final shove. Somewhere behind him, Askon heard a soft *click*, and then he was on his back in the hallway between the town hall's main chamber and the secret room. The hidden door swung back into place and clicked again. Askon picked himself up and reflexively brushed his pant legs.

He crossed into the large room, its walls barren and empty. His cloak hung near the fireplace, where he had left it the night before. He smiled and held it up in the shadowy room, his eyes moving first over the cloak, and then to the stone hanging from his neck: both green. Fitting, he thought, that the two should match. His mind began to drift, back to the fair morning when he had received the cloak. It had been a gift. But he was interrupted. The clicking came again, quieter this time, then a soft swish. A moment later, Morrowmen appeared at the end of the chamber, his weight supported by the short prop which Askon remembered all too well.

The old man hobbled slowly toward the fireplace where Askon stood wrapping the cloak about his shoulders. "Is everything alright?" he asked, adjusting the clasp.

"She will be fine," said Morrowmen softly. "But the healing process isn't without effort on my part. Periodically, for the near term anyway, she will need treatment from me." He cleared his throat and lowered himself gently onto a block of firewood. "Soon I will have no choice but to move her. My men are on their way to help with the task. We will all be much safer if we leave this place. I don't fully trust that Iramov will not return, especially when he discovers that his scepter is nothing more than a gorgeous decoy."

Askon turned to Morrowmen. "Are you suggesting that I go with you?" He backed away. "No. My loyalties lie with the king. I cannot go. *My* men are, as we speak, on the run from a massive Norill force. And they have a weapon we have not seen before. They wield the same will-crushing darkness as Iramov. It's worst when used on new recruits and the weaker officers. I must warn the king. The Norill could be marching on the city in a matter of days."

While Askon defended his responsibility to the king's army, Morrowmen once again produced the pipe. By the time Askon had finished, he was already expelling the first cloud of smoke. "Too bad that rock around your neck doesn't confer an increase in cognitive ability. Are you listening to yourself? There are Norill with the same power as Iramov. Do you happen to know anywhere they might acquire it?"

"They are strange creatures. Perhaps it is some inborn magic?" said Askon.

Morrowmen scowled. "Listen to yourself. How often has the same thing been said about your kind?"

Askon's hands were at the old man's throat in an instant. "How dare you compare me to them?!" He squeezed hard, hoping for a reaction: fear, anger, obedience. Morrowmen only stared back, his sunken eyes wreathed in smoke.

"A fool will be compared to other fools," he said, prying Askon's fingers away. He was surprisingly strong, and though Askon's anger would have squeezed the withered neck tighter, the hand came free. "Ask yourself this," Morrowmen said. "Who else has used a power similar to this Norill weapon?"

Askon trembled slightly. His thoughts felt thick and sluggish. "Iramov?" He answered dumbly.

Morrowmen nodded, the end of his pipe swirling through the smoke. "The real question for you is how he could be both near enough to the Norill to wield the power himself or somehow dispense it to those vile creatures, while at the same time be here in Tolarenz."

"That's impossible."

"You said the same of my age not so long ago. Before you leave, wherever you decide to go, I have two suggestions. Well, they're assignments really, but I have no control over what you do after you leave this place. Follow them or don't; it is your decision to make."

"Go on," said Askon skeptically. Whatever Morrowmen wanted him to do would likely be the same as what Caled would advise. If nothing else, Askon would hear the old man out.

"First, before you leave the valley, I need you to send a signal to my men. Take this," he handed Askon the looking glass from the hidden room. "Use it to send a series of flashes toward the western side of the hills entering the valley. Just keep sending the flashes until you see a response. And you'll no doubt desire to investigate your parents' house before you depart; my men will see the signal from there."

"Alright," said Askon. "That seems simple enough."

Morrowmen smiled, nodding. "I had no doubt that you would do it. I'm too closely tied to Caled for you to see me as anything but an ally. Another fault in your intellect, but we have no time for education now." He lifted the tip of the pipe to a point below his eye, scratching absently. "Besides, you'll need that blind trust to complete my second suggestion, though the proof will be easy enough to see once the task is complete." The pipe tip crawled up the cheekbone to the temple and crossed into the sparse eyebrow. "Go back to your king," said Morrowmen, "but first find your friend, Edward. Warn them both of the coming Norill threat. Reveal as little as possible concerning the events you have seen here."

A wounded look sprang onto Askon's face. "I heard the story," he said, and his voice boomed in the hall. "I've been entrusted with something secret, something important. I will not reveal it." Then he heard the whistling, but the old man's cane halted in midair, just before impact.

"Good," said Morrowmen. "Shouting about it, however, isn't the best way to keep a secret."

Askon laughed uncomfortably, his eyes still on the cane. Morrowmen lowered it and continued, "Tell your friend more than you tell his father, however. Listen to what he has to say; learn from him."

"You're asking that I use a friend for reconnaissance?"

Morrowmen hesitated, then nodded. The pipe stopped its wandering, and the brilliant eyes glimmered like sharpened knife-points in their sunken sockets. "Something is going on between those two, Iramov and Codard. I have a hypothesis, but you don't fully trust me yet. Just don't let it become a maze of endless self-questioning as Caled so often did. Go there. Find out how the two are connected. I would say 'trust no one', but that is said too often in such cases, and I'm asking you to trust me, so it would seem counterproductive."

Askon let his head fall back, his eyes traveling along the barren walls. He tried to recall each missing piece of art, every chair and table, but they had already begun to fade. The prominent works, like *The Raising of a City*, still remained in his memory, but the less important were gone. Should he trust this man: a man who had appeared so mysteriously, speaking of children's fairytales as if they were historical accounts? So many times, such strangers had captivated their listeners only to reveal wicked purposes when the target's defenses relaxed. But Askon had seen Iramov's work with his own eyes, seen the pulsing, blood-red stone, felt the press of the darkness, and it was the same as that used by the Norill. He looked back to Morrowmen. "On the first request, you have my word. As for the second, I need time to think. The more information I can provide to the king, the better our chances for success against the Norill," he said. Silently he considered the consequence of revealing too much if Codard really was in league with Iramov.

"You'll do the right thing," said Morrowmen, rising from the block of firewood. "In that at least, Caled chose well."

Askon was already halfway across the main chamber toward the door. In the shadows a faint green light radiated from the fragment at his chest. It cast a soft glow around his silhouette in the semi-darkness. He opened the door, and the green vanished in a blaze of white sunlight. Before crossing the threshold Askon turned to Morrowmen, calling back into the hall. "If you're right," he said, "how will I find you again?"

"You won't," Morrowmen barked. "If I'm right, and let's face it, I almost always am, take Edward to the South Kingdom. Lord Apopsé knows where to find me. And put that fragment under your clothes! It's like a green beacon to anyone who knows what they're looking for."

Askon tucked the gem under his shirt. He pulled the hood of his cloak over his head and closed the heavy wooden door. Wind whispered in the trees and flowers of the garden. On a branch a few feet above his head, Marten perched, motionless. The falcon alighted at Askon's shoulder, and they turned from the well-worn path, plunging into the dense garden toward his parents' home, wary of the possibility that Iramov had left spies behind.

Askon crept through the vacant village. When he had arrived, the quiet had been merely unsettling; now it was eerie. The hanging metal baskets in Roland's garden creaked as the wind pushed them back and forth. Voices should have filled the air: townspeople chatting with friends and family, but they did not. The ping and clank of the forge should have rung along the wood-paneled houses, but the smithy was silent. Laughter, possibly even a song, should have drifted from within the houses lining the street. Not now.

He checked every corner, sighted every line throughout the town. But in all his vigilance, he was unable to locate a single living person. Marten circled above, giving no indication that Askon's conclusion should be cast into doubt. With the sun descending upon the encircling mountains, Askon rounded the western side of his parents' home, closing in from the back. He climbed the hill, and the house appeared over the crest: roofline, upper windows, terrace, lower windows, back door, his father's porch, and the little trees.

Approaching the rear of the building seemed the best way to enter unseen in the case that Iramov had left sentries to guard the valley's entrance. Askon's house would be the perfect location: outside of town, two stories, on a small hilltop. He neared the porch silently, the green cloak rendering him nearly invisible amongst the grasses and small trees which now lay scattered over the workspace behind the house. Then in one of the upper windows a tiny ripple of motion disturbed the otherwise complete stillness. Instantaneously, Askon was at the door, turning the handle, through the kitchen, up the flight of stairs, standing—sword drawn and ready—at the entrance to his parents' bedroom. In all, it seemed only a few seconds from the field behind the house to the doorway on the second floor. They were still there, Iramov's men, in his house, and he would make them pay.

He kicked the door open, splintering the makeshift lock, nearly ripping the door from the hinges. When he stepped through, Iramov's man was already upon him. Sword strokes rained down wildly and Askon retreated a few steps into the hallway. The attacks came quickly, unnaturally so, and Askon immediately recognized the poor swordsmanship in their delivery. But they poured on, Askon's drive to attack subdued in the effort to parry and avoid his opponent's inhuman speed. Rage boiled inside Askon, and as the anger grew, the blows only increased in frequency.

"What are you?" Askon screamed, but the response came only in more sword strokes. They sliced so quickly through the air that Askon could no longer track them. And though he followed the arms and body to block the attacks, they were too many and too fast. Askon's guard faltered, and the opposing blade cut through the leather at his right bicep and into the skin. Blood flowed from the wound, and Askon remembered the powdered circle.

"Get out of my house!" he shouted again. His blade and the other slammed together, the speed of his opponent too great. Askon's sword held, while the other cracked and broke a few feet from the hilt. A painful vibration shot through Askon's hand, and his sword fell from his grasp with a clatter. The broken blade flashed down. Askon roared, catching the man's hands at the wrists and driving him backward through the door, into the bedroom. The shattering of glass filled Askon's ears as he screamed, twisting the weapon back toward his attacker. When they reached the ground, Askon's weight drove the blade into the man's chest. He jumped up, panting over the corpse.

The sun drifted lower, plunging toward the horizon. A shadow lay, stretching ever longer on the grass. It did not move. Its tense, rigid shape communicated without sound or word the anger, the hatred that seethed from the figure to which it was inextricably connected. Askon stared down at the body.

Shards of glass glittered in the remaining light, a halo of inconsequential stars around the constellation of a dead man. The face, young and inexperienced, had relaxed into the peaceful posture of death. It was not a smile, nor was it a grimace of rage as was Askon's. Had he drawn this lot: to stay behind and scout the valley? Was he ranked low enough to be forced to remain when his commanders had fled? Perhaps he had seen a moment of opportunity, a chance to advance his position by undertaking a dangerous assignment—the way Askon had done when he rescued Edward. Or had this man found enjoyment in the emptiness of the half-elven city? Askon turned from the body, gripping the bleeding wound on his own right arm. Tears streamed down his face. He let them fall.

"Askon?"

"Yes Liana."

"Uh…Um…"

"Well, are you going to ask or not?"

"What's it like to kill somebody?"

"Líana! Why would you ask me that? You shouldn't be thinking of such things."

"I know. It's just, you go fight for the king, and I know what that means. So, what is it like?"

"You should ask Mother and Father. They may not want you to know, yet. Hopefully ever."

"Why! Because I'm a girl? Mother and Father said that killing someone is wrong, that it's evil, but you do it for the king's army."

"It's different. We're protecting you, and them, and everyone."

"If it isn't evil, then tell me what it is like."

"Alright. Give me your hand."

"Why?"

"Just do it."

"Ok…Ow! Why did you do that? Now my finger's bleeding."

"The needle point just killed a little part of you, in your finger. Did it hurt?"

"Of course it did!"

"Yeah, it hurt me too. Maybe more than it hurt you. Now you do it."

"No problem. Give me the needle."

"Not to me. Prick your own finger."

"But it will hurt!"

"That's what it's like, Líana. Only it's a much bigger needle. To take someone else's life, you have to be willing to give up part of yourself. Some

people learn to ignore it, like Mother ignores the needle when she sews. The strongest soldiers, the best men, they feel it every time."

The shadows continued to lengthen in the little green valley as the sun fell upon the mountains in the west. Leaving the body behind, Askon rounded the front of the house. He passed through the garden of stunted trees, recalling the hours that his father had poured into their grooming. At a glance they were only small, carefully pruned shrubs, but a less casual eye found personalities wholly unique in each of them. Askon lowered his hand, stretching out the fingertips, and brushed the needles of a miniature spruce. Its crooked limbs showed the evidence of many prunings, tiny lumps which had once been branches. His father had probably given it several titles in its lifetime: stubborn, willful, persistent, indomitable. How long had this tree survived? Askon was unsure, and he let the memory pass, leaving it and the tree behind as he stepped into the house.

Inside, the rooms were bare, gutted. Every wall blank, every piece of furniture absent. The kitchen had been stripped of all plates, knives, forks, rags, food. All the identifying material items which had given the house its sense of self were gone, just as those who had once lived there were gone. In the emptiness he listened to his own breathing, to the swish of his pant legs against one another. The house felt much larger with everything removed and its inhabitants evicted, or perhaps it was Askon who felt smaller.

He continued through the house and up the stairs. The second floor was as empty as the first. Askon peeked into his own bedroom and nothing, not a single item remained; even the heavy wooden bed frame had been extricated, probably by breaking it into pieces and heaving it out the window. Líana's room was the same, and so he proceeded down the hall to his mother and father's room. Inside, he saw the pointed edges of the shattered window flashing like fangs in the failing sun. He crossed the room in three quick strides—remembering his purpose—and fished through his belongings for the small mirror. Finding it, he lifted the reflective surface to a point level with his face. It had not been broken by the fall, as Askon had originally feared. However, a weary, weather-beaten traveler stared back, and he turned the mirror away.

He raised the looking glass to the window and twisted his wrist quickly: once, twice, three times. Then a pause. Once, twice, and again. He waited, then reproduced the series of flashes as Morrowmen had instructed. At first he thought the signal had been ineffective, and he began the sequence a third time. But then a response came: one, two, three, pause, one, two, three. Askon released the mirror and his breath, only now realizing that he had been holding both as he waited for the return signal. At the edge of his vision, so far that he wondered if a human could have even seen it at all, he recognized the signal a second time. It traveled north again and a burst of tiny glittering flashes flickered in the trees above the town hall. Morrowmen's followers had scattered themselves across the whole of the valley's western side. The number of signals originating near the hall filled Askon with assurance. Morrowmen and his patient would be well-protected. Askon turned from the window and made his way back down the stairs to the ground floor.

When he reached the landing at the bottom of the stairway, he allowed himself to pass through the kitchen one final time before leaving his home. Memories came haltingly, unclear, as the bare cupboards and counters did not reflect the images in his mind. He continued through the short hallway at the back of the house, onto the porch. There, he saw the tiny trees smashed and broken. Several pots had simply been shattered and left behind, too unimportant to be carried along the road to the fire. From one of the broken pots, the roots of a tree protruded. It was the healthy tree his father had most recently tended. Askon's eyes moved from its crumpled branches to the workbench. There, untouched, lay the half-dying twin of the healthier sibling in lonely defiance, watching over those which would never reach the garden. Askon smiled. The leaves had begun to sprout anew on the little tree, and their color was more vibrant than before. It was still sickly and pale in comparison to the others, but life thrived there.

He scooped the tree and its round pot into the crook of an arm and closed his eyes tightly. Squeezing the cool ceramic pot, he faced the house, opening his eyes once again to take in the sight of his childhood home. Backing away a few steps, he faded into the grass.

He emerged onto the path some half of the distance back through the desolate town. Marten busily circled the valley, a loftier sentry than Iramov's and silent as a thin breeze. When he returned again to rest on the leather shoulder guard, Askon knew that the area was clear of any threat. Now, bird on one arm, tree in the other, he marched past the houses and gardens to the center of town. He skirted the remains of the rain-soaked fire. Here and there, thin fingers of smoke curled up from beneath the charred shapes. As the large powdered circle appeared before him, Askon bowed his head. Between the garden and the circle, he left the ragged tree, the sun now only a sliver clinging to the rim of mountaintops. Through the garden and to the large wooden door of the hall Askon strode. There he entered the building.

"Morrowmen," he called. An echo returned. The main chamber had darkened in the time since Askon had left. He had come back to inform Morrowmen of the sentry, and to warn him that though Marten's sweep had shown the valley clear, spies could still be watching.

"Morrowmen!" he called again, only this time much louder. He crossed the main chamber and paced through the hallway to the hidden door. "There's something I need to tell you before I go," he shouted, one fist banging against the wooden panel. "Let me in."

The door did not open, and no sound came from the room within. Askon pawed at the wall on each side of the door, searching for the catch. In a groove to the right some three feet distant from the doorframe, he found the lever. It rested flush with the wall, but was not entirely seamless. He pulled down lightly on the wooden hook inside the groove and heard the distinctive *click* that would release the door.

Stepping into the secret room, Askon found the walls and floors bathed in warm orange light. The fading sun still cast its rays through the skylight, though it was now a dim glow rather than the brilliant shafts of the morning. "Morrowmen?" Askon said, not quite in a whisper.

The sheet on the floor was missing, as was the survivor beneath it. The food, of which Askon and Morrowmen had eaten the majority, had been swept up and removed. On the table the glass decanter still rested, as did Askon's cup, but the vessels were both empty now. Morrowmen was already gone.

When Askon returned to the garden, shadow had crept across the western side of the valley. The hall itself lay under the dark blanket, as did the garden and most of the square. Orange faded to blue and blue to black just above the peaks of the small mountain range. Askon lifted the hood of his cloak and proceeded through the quiet flowers to the powdered circle where the sickly tree lay, awkward and out of place only a few feet from the towering oaks that made up the entrance to the town hall garden. There, he lifted the pot over his head and smashed it against the ground just outside of the white ring.

With a sturdy ceramic shard in hand, he stepped across the threshold into the circle. He carried shard and tree to the center and gingerly lay the gnarled roots of the plant on the rain-softened earth. Then he drove the makeshift shovel into the dirt.

The fragment of Alora's Tear fell lightly from under his shirt to dangle openly on its silver chain. Green light pulsed against his hands and clothes. The ceramic pierced the thin white layer, but no tears came to Askon's eyes, and no anger welled within him. Time seemed to slow nearly to a halt, and he pushed the shovel into the ground again. The light behind the mountains ceased to fade and instead hung suspended in twilight. All around the garden, the swaying oaks slowed their delicate movements as though the trees and grass were suddenly submerged at the bottom of a great sea. Askon brought the shard down again and again, until he was satisfied with his work.

He placed the tiny tree in the center of the powdered circle, scooping excess dirt into the hole and pressing it firmly down. When he was finished, he raised his eyes. The first star appeared, twinkling brightly in the east, and the valley stood in reverent stillness.

Acknowledgements

It's funny. Many readers reach the back of the book only to discover the Acknowledgements, ignore them, and go on wondering about what comes next in the story. That's all well and good. What author wouldn't want readers to be left wondering? But what that reader doesn't know is how much work went into the production of the book they've just finished. Without the countless hours of reading, rereading, discussing, and note-taking, there would be no story, no Askon, no Thomas, no John.

So it is my honor to thank those who helped in the writing of this book. To my wife Kelli, who has supported this project more than anyone else would have the good sense to. Weekends, vacation days, every spare minute I could scrape together, she was there to take care of children, bring up the occasional coffee, and endure endless ramblings concerning the world of Vladvir in spite of *Harry Potter* being the only fantasy series she has ever read. And to Mom, because what person in their right mind doesn't thank her, and because when no one else would read the story, she did. The first wrinkles were smoothed out according to her observations, and many more were discovered on her watch and dealt with accordingly. To Dad for telling me what should have been obvious (sometimes I just need to hear it from you). To my friend, Scott Boren, a kindred fantasy reader and the first outside of the familial circle to finish the story. You offer a perspective I hadn't hoped to find amongst my non-internet helpers. I know you're awaiting part, the next. It is coming, I assure you.

To my teachers: Mrs. JoAnne Johansen for assigning the project that inspired a world and a series and so much more fifteen years later; Rick Fehrenbacher for the Tolkien class that introduced me to "On Fairy Stories," the text that drove much of the first draft; and Joy Passanante for reminding me that teachers can love their jobs, do them well, and still create works of their own.

To my editor, Zoë Markham, for being the right person at the right time with the right perspective. And to my cover and map artist, Isis Sousa, for the exceptional honor of seeing my imagined people and places come to life. It is still so strange (and wonderful) to see Askon looking back at me.

And to everyone else who helped at some point along the way, either by reading a draft, acting as a sounding board, or generally being a cheerleader on my behalf: Adam Morgan, Andi Arnold, Jen O'Connor (without whom I would never have read *Song of Ice and Fire*), Rachelle Gilbert, Atticus Faul, Matt Hally, Jaime Tidwell, Katie Rigby, Brian Winterbottom, Scott Zarder, Julie and Emily Skinner, Kate Patterson, and Erin Faulk.

Thank you all so much. And thanks to the readers, whether you made it this far or stopped in the quiet valley with Askon.

Continue the Journey

Askon returns with news of Iramov's treachery. John confronts the Norill at Austgæta. And Thomas sounds the alarm, warning Vladvir's outposts of the coming darkness.

Pre-order Alora's Tear: Book 2 now.

barhamink.com/vol-2

About the Author

Nathan spends most of his working days with the students of Genesee Junior-Senior High School in Genesee, Idaho. Whether it's essay structure, a classic literary work, or the occasional impromptu dance routine, he strives to keep students interested in the fun and the fundamentals of the English language.

When he's not teaching, he wears a number of hats, though the one that says "Dad" is the most careworn and cherished (it says "Husband" on the back). It hangs on a hook in a house where music is a constant and all the computers say "Apple" somewhere on their *aluminium* facades. From time to time it is said that he ventures into the mysterious realm called *outside*, though the occasion is rare and almost exclusively upon request by son or daughter.

Sign up for Nathan's newsletter:
barhamink.com/subscribe

Connect with Nathan:
Twitter: twitter.com/natebarham
Blog: natebarham.com

CPSIA information can be obtained
at www.ICGtesting.com
Printed in the USA
FSOW01n1435241114
3565FS